Adult Nature

Copyright 2020 Matthew Licht & HST

Cover design by Manlio Bigeschi

Horror Sleaze Trash

www.horrorsleazetrash.com

TABLE OF CONTENTS

I Am Rocco Siffredi

When I woke up, I was Rocco Siffredi. What does Rocco Siffredi eat for breakfast? He does not eat breakfast. He goes out and looks for something to fuck. The first thing I saw was a chick with big tits. So I went up to her and whipped it out. She got on her knees, right there in the street. "Suck," I said. "Suck hard." She sucked. She sucked hard.

A cop saw what we were doing, and thought it was obscene or indecent or some stupid shit like that. Cops must not fuck enough, or they'd leave people alone. The cop said, "Hey! You can't do that here! Go make a porno movie or something."

"I'm Rocco Siffredi," I said. "My life is a porno movie. What're you gonna do? Arrest me for living my fucking life?"

To show the cop I meant business, I pulled out and sprayed my co-star's cheekbones. Then I wiped off on her hairdo and moved on.

Before I was Rocco Siffredi, I seem to remember I had a job, like in a bank or some shit. But now that I was Rocco Siffredi, I went into the bank to fuck. I pushed everyone in line aside. Rocco Siffredi does not wait in line. The teller was African-American.

"Hey," I said. "You ever see a soul brother with a dick this big?"

She gasped and pulled up her skirt. I slammed it right in.

The man who used to be my boss before I was Rocco Siffredi came out of his office. "What's going on out here?" He saw what I was doing to my new banker girlfriend. "You're fired!"

Then he pointed at me.

"You!" he hissed. "You're double-fired!"

He was always such a bossy fucking boss, but now I was Rocco Siffredi. Nobody bosses Rocco Siffredi. I hosed down my former boss from my former stupid life.

Glazing that idiot with sperm made me hungry. I barged into a steakhouse and got some steaks. I fucked the waitress for the check. She wanted to give me her tip money, but I'm not a whore. I am Rocco Siffredi, porn star supreme!

When the sun went down, I went to a disco. Not just any disco—the most exclusive disco in town. Make that, the world. The velvet rope knew enough to get out of the way.

A supermodel appeared. She said, "Fuck me hard, Rocco!"

Supermodels like to live dangerously.

Gently, I grabbed her ears. My gunk shot out her nose. It was beautiful.

"What the hell are you doing?" someone said. "It's past your bedtime and you gotta go to work tomorrow!"

Shit. That voice sounded familiar.

Before I was Rocco Siffredi, I think I had a wife, somewhere.

She was standing in the disco doorway. She had a bottle in her hand. She's good with a bottle. I dropped the supermodel. She fell limp to the unmopped disco floor.

My wife approached. She held the bottle by the neck. She holds me that way sometimes. She broke the bottle against a glittery railing.

My life as Rocco Siffredi was over.

Sucked Into the Cult

Harry Doss was in a foul mood when he got off the flight from Houston. Fat passengers had crowded him from both sides. Infants shrieked in the rows ahead and behind. A stewardess spilled coffee in his lap. Aside from the pain and the un-businesslike stain, his cell-phone was ruined in the accident. The plane landed nearly two hours late.

He fumbled his pockets outside a phone booth in the Arrivals zone. He didn't have enough change to make an urgent call. Harry was about to miss the most important meeting of his career.

A hooded figure swathed in sunset hues chose this moment to approach.

Out of the corner of his eye, Harry Doss saw someone shove a book in his face. He wanted to lash out, or at least be verbally abusive. But when he saw her, he was paralyzed and struck dumb. He forgot his business appointment. He forgot his struggling electronics corporation. He wanted to kneel, surrender his soul and devote himself to the most beautiful woman he'd ever seen.

"Have you accessed the godhead today, sir? For a small donation, the Ultimate Truth can be yours. If you would only give me a few minutes of your valuable time, I can explain..."

Oh Hell yes. Harry Doss put down the germ-laden receiver he'd intended to use as a bludgeon. Instead of telephone change, he pulled business expense cash from his pocket. Twenty, forty, sixty bucks was a small price to pay for Ultimate Truth. Each additional banknote made the woman who was proof of God's existence to shake and jiggle in surprised delight.

Harry Doss went from harried businessman to horny Everyman, eager to cheat on his wife.

Betty-Sue Doss was a good homemaker. He'd kept his promise to forsake all others, but the godhead had given a sign that his fast must end.

Harry and the cult woman went to sit in a quiet spot. She opened the book Harry had so expensively bought to a picture of a bald-headed, prune-faced gentleman with flowing gray nose-hair.

"This is Swami Vishnaswoti." She sighed at the name, pulling back the hood of her orange sweatshirt.

Harry looked to see whether she was blonde or brunette, and was shocked to discover she was as bald as the dude in the picture. He pictured her nude, being shaven by other saffron-robed figures in some initiation ritual, with muted drums and a droning chant.

If there was a God, Harry wondered, why should some codger with excess nose-hair get to stare at, and probably fondle, his most glorious creation.

Harry's previous attempts at infidelity were a history of failure. Women he met on business trips and at conventions always declined his invitations to come back to a hotel room for meaningless, wonderfully mechanical adultery. One of them, when he asked her why not, said, "Oh, come on, darling. You're the kind who always says, 'I can't do this. I love my wife.'"

What followed was a kiss that made Harry Doss wonder what might've been for months.

'*This* time,' he thought, 'it's not going to go that way.'

He dropped his voice to interrupt the flow of Swami-blab.

"What's your name, young lady?"

"Kryst...I mean, Davadip."

"I'm Harry. Listen, what you're telling me is just what I wanted—needed—to hear. Our meeting is no coincidence, it's synchronicity. I'm in a spiritual crisis. I'm lonely, Davadip. Lonely and scared of what lies ahead. Perhaps you and Swami..."

"Vishnaswoti."

"...can relieve a troubled soul."

Sales meetings be damned. Hello, bankruptcy court. Goodbye, wife and kids. Harry Doss, minor-league business manager, was gonna nab himself some cult cunt.

They exited the airport and got into a cab.

"Kranepool Hotel," Harry told the turbanned, bearded taxi driver. "Step on it."

Harry's head buzzed with visions of nude Davadip in a hotel shower stall.

"Wait a minute," she said. "Oh my God mister, I

didn't say I was going to a *hotel* with you." Davadip sounded like she was about to cry.

Harry Doss felt his spirit drain. "Oh I'm sorry. Of course not. But I swear I only want to talk to you. Tell me where we could go instead."

"Driver, take us to the Ashkanoma Ashram. It's at the end of Crapper Boulevard."

But the driver refused to go to that outlandish address unless he got extra cash up front. Harry took out his wallet and was bled further. He'd have a tough time explaining these additional expenses, on top of the missed conference.

They entered a bad neighborhood. Texas Prisons looked more inviting than the Ashram. Davadip, however, sighed happily when she saw her home.

"Hurry up and get out," the cab driver said. He threw the car into reverse and was gone.

On the dirt driveway, Harry was surrounded by hulking men in orange hooded sweatshirts. Their faces boded ill.

"Rama-lama, brothers," Davadip said. "I've passed out all my tracts, gathered my donation quota, *and* I've brought a new truth-seeker to visit. Uhm, mister? I forgot your name."

"Harry. Pleased to meet you guys, but I think I gotta go..."

He stuck out his hand for shakes that never came. Gruff voices muttered words of friendship and welcome. Strong arms embraced him, and dragged him towards the tumbledown shack made to look like some hillbilly's idea of the Taj Mahal.

In a candle-lit darkness that reeked of incense and sweat, Harry Doss was relieved of his briefcase, then his clothes. "Hey! Knock it off!"

He stopped struggling when he saw he was being lightened and stripped by Davadip and several of her cult Sisters. Davadip looked into his eyes. "Relax," she said. "Let go. Let it happen."

She unzipped her sweatshirt. Harry's mouth hung open at the sight. There was even a trickle of drool. Here body was a milky white expanse, like a glimpse of the distant Himalayas.

"Oooh look, sisters. He's in need," one of the cult women whispered.

"Wouldn't he like to join with us," said another, pushing her bosom together.

"But he's not ready yet."

"Aw, poor guy. Let's give him a taste."

Eyes can only open so wide, but Harry's tried to break the World Record. Davadip's squeaky voice split the air.

"Wait, sisters! *I* found him. That means I get to minister to him first..."

Her eyes glowed with spiritual love and bliss.

Harry Doss thought he'd died and gone to Heaven, or Nirvana, whichever was heavenlier. His brain turned itself off. He reverted to a primitive state.

"Glaah...Baaah....Phlurgle..."

Davadip eventually moved aside and let her sisters join in. What was left of Harry's brain exploded. He saw pink visions of the Holy Ecstasy Beyond.

"That's enough, for now," said the senior shaven-headed Den Mother, zipping up her sweatshirt. Harry nearly broke down at the assertion.

"Bluh! Duh! Noooo!" He felt a hooded sweatshirt being pulled over his head.

"Time for you to grovel before Swami Vishnaswoti, o luckiest brother."

"Oh it'll blow your mind." Davadip planted a chaste kiss on Harry's cheek.

The men of the cult dragged him away with his orange drawstring pants around his ankles.

They dumped him on the rough floor in a dungeon rank with body odor. He heard a low hum, felt himself observed through the blackness. Someone struck a match and lit a candle, then several others. Harry saw the face of Swami Vishnaswoti.

He was even more wizened than in the photo Davadip had shown him. The Swami had grown a white mustache, Harry thought. Then he saw it wasn't a mustache at all, but the most luxuriant nose-hair in the history of the world. The Swami's eyes were hypnotic.

"Uh, hello," Harry said, and instantly felt a sharp smack to the back of his head.

"Silence before the Heavenly Master."

The Swami regarded Harry placidly. "You seem like a no-nonsense kinda guy," he said, with a heavy New York accent.

"Uh, sure. I guess."

"OK, I'm gonna level with you. We're on a holy mission here, but it's a business deal too. You start at the bottom and work your way up, through prayer and devotion to the cause. You hip?"

"Yeah. But..."

"Here's the deal: for every hundred bucks you bring in, you get five minutes with one of the girls–your choice. I mean, it's up to *her*, of course. You gotta get a sister's consent and approval first, but you'll find most of your new sisters to be quite *receptive*."

Harry was about to say, "But I've got a wife and kids and a job and..."

Another thought occurred. "Business, huh? What's in it for the girls? If this is some kind of brainwashing scam, I'm gonna call the cops."

"Relax, hero. They're in on the deal. For each C-note a sister brings home, she gets a personal worship-session. And for every dupe... that is, for every new *devotee* a girl converts, she gets to enjoy Holy Communion with the Master. And that's me, baby."

Harry snorted.

The Swami chuckled, his nose hair twitched.

"How 'bout a little demonstration? Been a slow day. Brother Hasham, go fetch Sister Davadip. This dude's not official yet, but let's say he counts."

"Yeah, o master."

The Swami slowly unwound himself from his lotus position. "Feel free to join in," he said. "With the chant, I mean."

The drone grew louder. Harry's eyes adapted to the eerie candlelight.

A sitar twanged. Muffled drums beat. Harry Doss thought of the business conference going on without him, of his wife Betty-Sue living out her daily routine. Then Davadip entered the basement and Harry thought no more.

"O Divine Teacher, thank you for this most sublime opportunity."

The Swami gave a curt wave. "Shake it, baby."

Davadip began to dance. Her sweatshirt fluttered in the air as she leapt and flew all around. By the time she finally bared it all, there wasn't much left of Harry Doss besides a pile of volcanic ash.

Dewy with sweat, Davadip approached the Swami.

Vishnaswoti leaned back against a brocade cushion and let his devotee have her way.

The chant grew louder.

"Rama-lama! Looba-gabba!"

Harry Doss joined in like a zombie.

"Rammalamma! Loobagooba!"

The show was disappointing. If Harry Doss had been in his ordinary state of mind, he would've thought, 'Big deal.' But Harry Doss wasn't in his ordinary state of mind. He was chanting at the top of his lungs.

You might see Harry Doss—he goes by Hare Das these days—at an airport or a street corner near you. His eyes shine with missionary zeal. He is a forceful proselytizer. The first time he brought a hundred dollars back to the Ashram, Davadip told him she knew he could do better. So he's working on bringing in a cool thousand. He knows he'll get to Heaven one of these days. The Master told him so.

The Essence

"Cancer," the doctor said.

Silence fell upon the room.

"Where is it, Doc?"

"Where's what?"

Maybe he thought I meant, the Truth, the Meaning of Life, the gold. Even if he knew, he wouldn't tell me.

"The cancer," I said.

"It'd be simpler to tell you where it's not: The reproductive system."

High school biology was a long time ago.

"Could you please be more specific?"

"The gonads. Genitalia. Your cock and balls."

He didn't say how much time was left, but the implication was clear: Not much.

Every human being wants to leave some trace of their existence behind. I should've painted a picture, or written a book, or welded some car-wrecks together. Too late now.

Life occasionally shows a sign. *This* is the Meaning. *This* is the Truth. *This* is where the gold is hidden. The sign next to The Sign said WE BUY GOLD $$$, but I had none to sell. I entered the sperm bank next door instead.

The reception desk nurse didn't even look up from her reading. She appeared quite engrossed in a supermarket tabloid with UFOs on the cover.

I cleared my throat several times.

She looked up, eyes glazed with wonder at the existence of heavenly beings who visit the Earth in sparkling streamlined spaceships. Instantly she could tell I wasn't one of them.

"What do you want?" she asked.

"This is a sperm bank, right? I want to donate."

She had a good laugh at this. "You?"

"Payment in cash, please."

Oh man, I slew her.

"We pay *some* donors," she said.

She opened a drawer in her desk, scrounged around for petty cash.

"How 'bout uh, two bucks and 73 cents?"

"Hand it over," I said. "I'll go get a burger first. For energy."

"We only pay on delivery, sir."

"Where's the delivery room?"

She jerked a thumb at a hospital-green curtain.

"Take some fantasy material," she said, shoving a worn dirty magazine across the desk.

"Listen," I whispered. "We could do this together."
"Huh?"

"Look, I don't need dirty pictures. I want you."

"What?"

"You're a nurse. You're supposed to help sick people, right? Well, I have cancer."

Her look said, *I bought this nurse outfit at the Salvation Army.*

"I'll bring you a hamburger when we're done," I offered. "Pleeeease?"

She thought about it for a moment, glanced around the empty waiting room.

"Got yourself a deal, mister."

The donation chamber stank of stale sweat and jissom. She shoved me in first, to prevent escape, and flicked on the light.

"Pull down your pants," she said.

I complied and she sniggered.

"Oh man, I've seen cock-a-roaches in here bigger than that..."

"Gets bigger," I said. "Open up your labcoat."

"You lay a finger on me, I'll put you in the emergency room."

I believed her. With the size of her arms, she could've KO'ed Sonny Liston. It was honestly kind of distracting.

I got busy working on myself. Nothing doing.

"Turn around," I said. "Hike your skirt and shake it."

She laughed at my request, but went along with it anyway.

It was warm in the donation chamber and getting hotter. I unbuttoned my shirt.

"Oh sweet Jesus," she said. "Have you ever even *thought* about taking a shower?"

"Hot water lowers the sperm count," I said. "Didn't they teach you that at Nurse College?"

"Hurry it up," she said. "Somebody else might come in."

"You want a rush job? Help me out."

She reached for my thing like it was a foaming rat. She grunted and tried to get it hard, or tear it off. Sonny Liston would've begged for mercy.

"Quit whining," she said.

"It's not gonna happen if you do it that way. Lube me up."

She hawked and spat.

"Hey! That's not what I..."

But her loogie proved magic.

"...oh, baby."

"Yeah I know that's why they hired me," she said.

"You're a goddess," I said. "Wish we coulda..."

"Shut up and concentrate. My wrist gets tired easy."

"Could I, like, touch you?"

"You wanna wind up in the morgue, go right ahead."

The lightbulb above us frazzled and went out.

"Hurry it up, fool," she said.

Holding back was never my strong suit anyway. The moment arrived, and she shoved me into the specimen tube and unclenched.

"Oooh-gah!"

The stuff of life squirted out of me and into the sterile plastic tube.

"I love you," I whimpered, collapsing against the wall.

"Sure. Now go get me that hamburger. I'm hungry."

Apparently, she didn't agree that what had just happened between us had been love.

But I fixed her. I ate both burgers myself.

The Anal Tits

Keli was walking down a New York street when she found an anus. She saw the anus in the gutter, the way seasoned bums spot quarters, but she didn't pounce the way bums do. She stopped, discreetly made sure no one was around, and bent down to pick it up. The anus was about the size of a quarter, pinkish-brown, slightly puckered. Keli couldn't tell if it was male or female.

Keli gave the anus a sniff. She didn't want to put anything dirty in her pocket or purse. The anus looked clean. If anything, it smelled faintly and pleasantly of almonds. Keli hadn't noticed any "Asshole-Scoop Killer Strikes Again!" headlines at the newsstands she'd passed recently.

A paperboy with a maroon turban on his head whistled at her. "Goodness me! Nice ass, Miss!"

That would've been enough to make it a good morning. Then she found an anus.

Things hadn't been going too well for Keli lately. She'd broken up with her boyfriend, whom she really liked. Actually, he broke up with her, which made it even worse. Then she got fired from her job at a restaurant because some asshole customer complained he saw Keli scratch her ass before picking up his order, and didn't stop by the washroom first to wash her hands with soap and water, as mandated by law. The customer said he was offended. He felt nauseated, he said, and not only refused to pay his bill but threatened a lawsuit. Keli was fired on the spot. OK, maybe she *had* scratched her ass. Everyone does, now and then. She hadn't scratched her ass on purpose, just to be gross. Besides, she kept her ass scrupulously clean. Keli was sure her ass was cleaner than most of the customers at Marlon's Fish Shanty.

Keli loved long, hot showers. She'd probe her rosebud with a soapy finger or two and feel it glisten, afterwards.

Keli was on her way to a job interview. There was an opening for a receptionist at a hot shot ad agency on Madison Avenue. She'd put on her most minimal mini-skirt. Her blouse was a white oxford-cloth button-down shirt from the Boys Department of a venerable menswear establishment, also on Madison Avenue. She wore it buttoned up all the way.

Keli had no bosom. She barely had nipples. Pencils laughed at her whenever she attempted the pencil test. Passing, in Keli's case, would've meant that the pencil found somewhere to stick for a change. The sound of pencils hitting the floor made Keli cry. Her tiny breasts swam around in padded A-cup bras from the Junior Misses department. Polite salesladies called Keli a "classic late-bloomer", but she'd given up hope that she'd ever develop. 'But I've got nice legs,' she thought, to console herself. 'And a great ass."

Keli had always led a rewarding sex life. She'd been introduced to anal sex by a caring, sensitive lover, a guy she'd met on a weekend trip to Miami. But Keli knew that bustlines were important, especially for receptionists. 'They're the first thing a client sees,' she thought.

'The clients won't be able to see my butt or legs 'cause I'll be behind the reception desk. *If* I get the job, that is.'

The starting salary was above average, and the Help Wanted ad said there were good opportunities for advancement. Advertising was an exciting field, and she wouldn't have to deal with finicky, neurotic restaurant patrons anymore.

Keli put the anus in her purse for good luck. 'God,' she thought, 'I really hope I get the job. I want this one, bad. I *need* it.'

Keli got the job. The nice man in charge of human resources at the ad agency said he liked her smile and her sincere, friendly, can-do manner.

The human resources guy was gay. Keli could tell because he was a bit too neatly dressed and groomed. He also wore a rainbow lightning bolt earring and a leather bracelet that said HONCHO in silver letters. But something about the gay human resources guy really turned Keli on. She almost asked him if he'd go on a date with her, despite his being gay.

'Now *there's* a guy who could appreciate my boyish figure,' she thought. 'Not like that jerk Derek who dumped me 'cause he wanted a girlfriend with big tits.'

But in the end, she decided asking the gay human

resources guy out on a date wouldn't have been professionally appropriate.

To celebrate her new job, Keli stopped by the feminist sex shoppe on her way home. The personable butch lesbian salesperson urged her to try out a new vibrator design called the Magic Bunny. When she switched it on, Keli heard a voice.

"Fuck the dumb bunny!" the voice said. "Go for the one with the anal probe. The anal probe, understand? The biggest they've got!"

"Excuse me?" Keli asked the salesperson.

"I said the bunny's ears flicker and flutter the clitoral hood and upper labia, as well as the clitoris itself. The missile-shaped design provides mild, non-aggressive, non-dominant penetration, to produce a satisfying holistic orgasm experience..."

"I thought you said, 'Fuck the bunny!'"

"Sister, if you're going to disrespect our merchandise, or if this is your idea of a male-type come-on, I'll have to ask you to leave our establishment."

"I must be hearing things. I'm sorry. Please give me the one with the anal probe. No, the bigger one."

"Uhm, this model requires a three-day waiting period. Just kidding! But seriously, what're you doing tonight? I mean, aside from...hey, just kidding!"

Keli thought her new black dildo-vibe looked like one of the threatening new nightsticks the cops were using lately. The instruction manual recommended water-based lube. *Lots* of water-based lube.

Fortunately, Keli had plenty of water-based lube back at home. She opened a bottle, plugged in her new toy, lay back, spread wide, and was just about to blast off when she heard, "Hey! What about me? Lemme outta here! I gotcha that job you wanted, didn't I?"

Keli thought, 'I got a job, but I'm losing my mind. Maybe it's because I masturbate to excess, or worry too much about my small bosom.'

"You want tits? Why'ncha just say so?"

The voice came from her purse. Keli remembered the anus she'd picked up. She went and got it.

"Okay, let's get busy, gorgeous."

"What? You're nothing but an anus."

"That's right. I am an anus. An anus is your boyfriend now."

The anus was masterful. Though a mere muscular ring of flesh, he loved her deep and hard. The anus understood Keli's animalistic desires. After a long, slow series of gut-wrenching orgasms and anal-gasms, Keli thought she really *had* lost her mind.

"Please, sweet anus," she begged. "I can't cum any more."

"Oh yeah? I was just getting warmed up. Listen, before you konk out, let's take care of your wish. There was something you wanted..."

"Tits! Oh, I want tits, anus. I want big ol', flopping tits!"

"Sure you do, kid. Same as any woman does. But you know the old saying: I do something for you, you do something for me. I guess you know what I'm talking about."

"Oh yes, lover. I mean...yes, anus. I'll do anything for you. Anything."

"You'd do it even if I *weren't* about to give you boobs, though, wouldn't you, Keli?"

"You know I would, anus. I'm all yours. You swim, I rim."

"Huh?"

"Oh, I dunno. It rhymes."

Keli said no more. She let her tongue do the talking.

Keli soon felt a tingle in her mosquito bite-size nipples. The fuzzy sensation spread to her armpits and ribcage. She licked harder. The anus moaned and cursed like a death row inmate. The swelling sensation in Keli's upper body grew. Keli groaned, and spread her legs. She was about to cum yet again. She pinched a nipple to boost her climax, and got a handful of tit.

Slowly, without missing a tongue-lash, she brought her other hand to her chest and felt another tit, just as big and full and warm and wonderful. For the first time in her life, Keli hefted and squeezed her massive boobs, pinching her outstretched nipples.

"Oh my God!" the anus cried.

You can guess what happened next.

Keli took a long, hot shower and felt good as new. Since she didn't own a bra, Keli didn't wear one on her first day at work. She put on the loosest boy-shirt she had, but still had to leave most of the buttons undone. Newsboys, construction workers and taxi drivers whistled and hooted as Keli sloshed and bounced and sashayed up and down the streets of New York. A cop made the international jack-off gesture with his nightstick.

"Hey, doncha know you could get arrested for showing off tits that big? Huh-huh-huh...just kidding. But not really, though."

The friendly gay human resources director at the ad agency took one look at Keli and tore off his gay earring and bracelet. He threw them in the nearest wastepaper basket. Then he tore off his shirt and tie and shredded his Stonewall T-shirt. His hairless chest rippled over 6-pack abs. He asked Keli out on a date, begged her not to take his request as sexual harassment or inappropriate, unprofessional behavior.

"Sure," said Keli. "I'd love to go out with you."

She didn't think he'd mind that she already had an asshole boyfriend.

In the Flush of Life

Wilma's apartment was full of rock n' roll junk. She'd balled some low-wattage stars, as a young groupie. Now her walls covered with obsolete concert posters and photos of dead musicians. The shelves were crowded with Elvis figurines and other pop collectibles.

Lucky Pete had been the drummer at a Sam the Sham revival show. That's how he met Wilma.

She still bore traces of flower-childhood, and some evenings Pete had nothing else to do except go visit her.

On the asshole-colored wall-to-wall carpet, at the foot of a scavenged couch, sat a plastic water-pipe and a huge black rubber dildo. Wilma smoked a lot of weed. Pete imagined her taking hits off her giant sex toy instead of the bong when she was stoned.

Marijuana fought an aerial duel with cat piss in her living room. It's been scientifically proven that feline fumes cause craziness in mature women. Wilma wasn't taking any chances, she was going to fry whatever was left of her brains between cat-piss and the pipe.

Pete preferred beer.

He nursed a brown glass baby-bottle, she made sexy sucking sounds with her water-pipe. Pete pointed to the dildo, which might've been art. "Where'd you find that?"

"A friend gave it to me."

"You ever use it?"

"Sure."

"How was it?"

"Great." She took a hit, held the smoke. A black cat knocked a Kung Fu Elvis statuette off the bookshelf with no books. Thanks to the thick carpet, it didn't break. The cat jumped down and went to the plastic basin next to the fridge. Wilma blew a Nagasaki cloud. "Taught me something about myself I didn't know."

"Like what?"

"Wanna watch?"

Pete shrugged. "I can't stand up."

Wilma hiked her suede miniskirt and went to work. A low-tide tang spread. A colorless fluid leaked.

"You just peed yourself a little," Pete said.

She looked hurt. "You think I'd do that in front of you like an animal?" She started in again with grim determination. She yelped and unplugged. A thicker liquid splashed onto the carpet.

"Wow," Pete said, but thought: 'She can't even tell the difference anymore.' The bottle in his hand was empty. "Listen, do you think you could get me another beer?"

She made it to the fridge, but stumbled on the catbox

and scattered its contents. Slug-trails gleamed on her thighs in the refrigerator light. Foam sprayed when she popped the cap. Frigid drops hit Pete's lap when she passed him the bottle.

"Thanks," he said.

Wilma sat back down and got busy again. She was warmed up.

Pete hoisted himself forward on the armchair.

A geyser blasted him back against the backrest.

He dried his face on his sleeve, polished off the beer. Wilma heaved, spent. The dildo fell to the floor with a muffled thump.

"Whudja think?" she said.

A white cat came and sniffed the rubber thing that smelled like the lady of the house, then went to piss on porcelain Elvis. He lifted his leg like a dog.

Pete had to take a leak too, but knew he'd never make it to the bathroom. He was holding an empty bottle. He unzipped and filled it, even overflowed a bit. "Whups, sorry."

Wilma pulled a face. "I think you'd better leave now."

Miracle In A Men's Room

One advantage of a religious education is a life-long obsession with sex. Eons later, I still remember Debbie Spinello.

A second-year girl, Debbie Spinello was secretly voted "Most Developed" at St J's Junior College.

The school had separate entrances for males and females. Demerits were handed out, penances assigned, for being out of uniform. So I was surprised when I ran into Debbie in the Young Men's room. She was smoking a forbidden cigarette, unfiltered.

"Wha-what're you doing in here?" I gasped.

Debbie Spinello exhaled a Bikini Atoll cloud, puffed a fleck of tobacco off her unfrosted lip (Holy Regulation #31B: Thou shalt not apply lipstick, nor lip gloss!) and said, "Duh. What about you?"

"This is the Young Men's Room. I need to urinate.

"Well, don't mind me. I ain't leavin' till I finish this butt."

But I couldn't leave. I was about to piss my pants. I approached the urinal. My hands shook when I unzipped. My penis was hard as an iron bar.

Debbie heard the silence, came over to see what was wrong.

"C'mon," she whispered smokily in my ear.

Mortified, I prayed for a quick, painless death.

"You're pee-shy? That's cute...Whoa! You got a fucking hard-on."

She punched my arm. I thought she'd report me to the Sisters. Holy Regulation #3 was: Thou shalt not never have a hard-on.

"We could, uh, not waste it," she said. "Know what I mean?"

Her cigarette sizzled when she flicked it into the urinal. Her slender fingers came together again, not in prayer. "Well I do, even if you don't."

"But...but...I gotta get back to class," I said. "Father Hurley's gonna send a patrol out for me in a minute if I don't..."

"Don't worry. This won't take long. First, you get it wet."

Debbie Spinello bent at the waist, and nearly hit her head on the cup of the urinal. The Fathers said that what she did was the worst thing that could ever happen, but it felt good.

When she stopped I didn't want her to. But then she said, "Wanna fuck?"

I nodded dumbly. "Too bad," she said.

My heart sank. The nuns had used Debbie as bait to trap a boy in his sinful lust.

"My folks have me checked once a week. Doc Snyder would report me for sure. He's my Dad's oldest buddy. Besides, I don't want to get pregnant. So you have to do my ass, OK?"

This time I nodded furiously.

"Unbutton me. I got a surprise for you."

She had to guide my hands. I fought the urge to rip and tear.

"Here silly, lemme show you how."

A gold medallion hung on a delicate chain in the hollow of her neck. Below was a heavy-duty white cotton bra. I grabbed.

"Be gentle," she whispered. "And warm your hands first. Ready for the surprise?"

Was Debbie Spinello really a boy? I'd heard stories from guys who'd been to Times Square. Was she an undercover cop? At that point, I didn't even care.

She unsnapped her bra and showed me the most beautiful things in the world. I wanted to start crying. But all I could say was, "So what's the surprise?"

That's when she tweaked her nipples.

"You got milk! You're lac...lactating! I thought you said you didn't wanna get pregnant?"

"I'm not pregnant, silly. It just happens. I thought it was a miracle at first, but I was too embarrassed to tell the Sisters. Doc Snyder says it's rare but normal. He said some Latin word, but I forgot. Mom has to buy me these special absorbent bras."

She knelt down and took me in her mouth. It was all too much.

"Do you like..."

Way too much. I nearly exploded, fell over

backwards. I thought she'd be angry.

"Wow," she said. "You must really like me."

"Oh Debbie," I moaned. "I love you. I always have. Do you know how often I've dreamed..."

She stood up and turned around, pulled up her skirt, pulled down her panties and braced herself against the wall over the urinal.

"You gotta spit on it first."

I went to clear my throat.

"Ew," she said, "not like *that*! You're supposed to, like, just drool on it a bit."

I did as she instructed and she reached around, guiding me in.

"Ow! Go slow! Go slow!"

So I went slow, even though I wanted to root around in Debbie like a warthog. To help keep my cool, I recited the Lord's Prayer backwards.

"Quiet," she said. "This feels really good, but we don't wanna get caught, do we?"

We did not.

"Milk me so I get off fast. But do it gently."

I pretended I was back on Uncle Olaf's farm in Wisconsin.

Debbie wrothe and squirmed. We fell against each other, crashed into the urinal. The thing flushed. We slid to the cold tile floor.

"Omigod," Debbie whispered. "I can't go back to class like this. You gotta help me out, OK?"

"Sure," I said. "What'm I supposed to do?"

"Clean me up," she hissed. "Come on, hurry."

She got on all fours.

Debbie tasted evil. When I was done, she whipped around so we could kiss.

The memory of that kiss lingers on and on.

Debbie wiped her mouth on my shirt, walked out of the Men's room and out of my life forever.

She got kicked out of school for smoking.

<u>Vodka Deodorant</u>

The woman in the fake leather suit looked exhausted. She had anemia or a timid form of albinism, accentuated by heavy makeup around her pale eyes. She stared at the supermarket cash register's conveyor belt as it rolled.

The guy who rang up her purchases attempted a pick-up line. He plucked his eyebrows. Gym muscles bulged under his supermarket smock.

Maybe she didn't understand Italian.

He didn't have time to try again, in another language. Her shopping list would've fit on a defunct communist country's postage stamp. Vodka and deodorant slid by, registered, clunked into the stainless steel merchandise holding pen. She refused the offer of a shopping bag for an additional six Euro-cents. She put the vibrator-shaped deodorant applicator in her pocket, grabbed the bottle by the neck and made to scat.

She didn't smash me with it when I asked to walk her home. Maybe she didn't understand German. Don't know why I thought she might.

I didn't offer to carry her no-logo bottle. She'd have thought I planned to steal it.

On the way out of the supermarket's glare, we walked past lost-looking old folks taking advantage of free unnatural warmth.

Heat was included with the rent in New York, as was hot water. Felt like warmth and personal hygiene were free.

The generic neighborhood was identifiable only by streets named for pre-European Union countries. Maybe she caught the irony of winding up on Soviet Union Street. Maybe irony was a luxury concept she didn't understand. Spike heels hobbled her wiggle along the crumbling sidewalk.

Vodka had been a problem in the former USSR. Dictators launched USA-style prohibition, restrictive rationing, scorched-earth surtaxes. Soviet drunks turned home-brewed beer into instant vodka with a dash of mosquito repellent. They slathered shoe polish on rye bread and left it on the radiator for delirious LSD-like trips. I asked her if she mixed generic deodorant and no-logo vodka for a narcotic effect.

Vodka was to drink, she said. Deodorant was for stink. I asked if she was a prostitute. She nodded and said I was one too, as if I didn't know.

"Look, I've got some food in my backpack," I said. "Let me make you dinner. Nothing fancy. No-logo spaghetti, but it tastes pretty good."

She wasn't sure she had a spaghetti pot. She'd rented a room in an apartment from people she barely knew, but hadn't inspected the kitchen cabinets. She didn't say no.

Cheap euro-architecture guarantees maximum winter

cold. Construction speculators were mobbed up with gas-heater factories, and the natural gas and oil industries. Her place was warm. Her former-Soviet Union flat-mates stole heat from somewhere else.

She took off her jacket, released an alcoholic reek as faint as a capped bottle of evil perfume waved slowly under the nose.

Her armpit-hair was the color of straw. She sat on a rickety chair to watch. No chopping block. No spaghetti pot. No can-opener, but that was no problem because generic tomato-pulp cans have futuristic pop-top tabs these days. Dull little knife couldn't peel an apple. Luckily, bargain brand tuna cans are packed with enough low-grade olive oil to lubricate a sauce. She pulled a loose no-logo cigarette from her purse, bumped me aside to light up at the stovetop. That was as close as she ever got to cooking.

Someone else was in the apartment. This phantom presences manifested different tobacco smells, muffled burps, sighs, wheezes. TV drone oozed through the thin walls. Human breezes moved scorch-marked curtains. Behind them, dirty windows faced a cement courtyard crowded with junked motor-scooter parts, corroded metal garbage bins. A cat prowled across the scene, evicted or escaped from some similar desolation. An invisible dead cat looked smug under a fogged plastic sheet.

"Where you from?"

She had to think. Wasn't used to direct questions. More accustomed to evasive action when direct questions were asked. Where you from what're you doing here where's your entry visa and residence permit? But immigration cops don't offer free spaghetti. She was from an unpronounceable war-torn town in Kosovo. She politely repeated her name, but I couldn't imitate the sounds. She didn't ask who I was or where I was from or what I was doing. She thought she knew what I wanted. In other words, same as everyone. But she was wrong. Unless the shower worked.

And money's been a problem since the dirty magazine biz tanked.

Being dirty is no longer a viable commercial asset.

She frisked my knapsack, found the bargain chocolate, had dessert before the starch course. She was missing molars. Ashtrays of premature death breezed through her pale lips.

Dinner was payment enough for what she had to offer. We hit the shower first. Practically had to demonstrate the proper use of bargain brand soap and dental floss. We toweled off in the low-consumption neon-bulb mist.

"Get the deodorant you bought. Bring the vodka too."

She went.

Hot water accentuates alcoholic buzz. Maybe I took a swig of deodorant after she slathered her armpits. The stuff foamed like shampoo, tasted about the same. I remembered the cheapo razors among my recent supermarket purchases. I still shaved, occasionally. So I left her under a stream of hot water and tromped to the kitchen.

Bumped into another woman in the dark hallway. She smelled like she was from Bukovina, or Bucharest, Burkina Faso, Montenegro, Sierra Leone, Bophuthatswana. Human flotsam status cuts through and across geo-political boundaries. She walked around without light due to inflated electric bills, or else she was so stoned that low-watt neon hurt her eyes. She flinched when she lurched into a stranger.

I returned to the bathroom.

She was staring at the medicine cabinet over the sink. Where am I? Who am I? What am I doing? Why am I alive? Clouded mirrors don't reflect answers to such easy questions. The tile floor was slippery. The cold outside the bathroom window wanted in, and was making headway. She came back into the shower unquestioningly. I shaved with deodorant foam. She shaved her legs to fully exploit the free razor.

Mouldy towels, unmade stale bed. The window in her room had a rolling metal shutter, stuck in the down position for complete blackout. She kept up her zombie act until I spoke. Can't remember what I said. Normal phrases from everyday human intercourse in a language not her own.

Humping drunks who mutter words she didn't understand must've been an overly familiar unpleasant situation.

She didn't go berserk in the usual manner. She unleashed an inbred reverse-pheromone bio-weapon. I went limp and rolled away.

She lit a cigarette butt stashed between the lumpy

mattress and the floor. Lime-green no-logo lighter, the kind sold by roving Africans, flash-lit a room filled with empty bottles. She held fire like Lady Liberty, scrounge-searched for a phallic deodorant applicator that still had some of the whitish liquid inside, rolled it under her arms. Vodka bottles and deodorant applicators hugged the walls in disorderly rows, stood crowded in the corners, lay scattered on the dirty floor and ugly furniture. Two bottles a day keeps the undertaker away.

But not forever.

Who undertakes the removal of deceased illegal immigrants? Unaccounted corpses, stuffed in weighted logo-stamped supermarket bags, dumped in the river. Garbage-dump fires, distorted reflections of pyres by the Ganges, illuminate unattended non-ritual funerals. Only the river complains, to deaf imaginary ears. Dogs and contaminated carp get fat on the heels of dead dictators.

I zipped back into the mildewed bathroom, pulled on my damp clothes fast. Money was missing from my pants, but the thieving gypsy woman in the hall had left the documents and house keys. No use stealing keys unless they lead to quick burglary or auto theft. The address printed on my expired driver's license is half a world away.

How Mrs. Steinmetz Got Her Mink

Every day on her way home from work, Mrs. Steinmetz stopped in front of the shopwindow of Vanderbolt Furs. Beyond the plateglass, mannequins stood frozen in elegant poses, swathed in ocelot, seal, beaver, chinchilla, ermine, but most of all, mink. Mrs. Steinmetz would stare at them until a truck engine would backfire, or some workman would shout, and the near-frozen woman would awaken from her trance to walk the rest of the way back to her dimly lit tenement, braving the winds which howl down big city streets.

Dinner was usually a can of soup heated up on the radiator. Mrs. Steinmetz listened to the radio while she ate, and she often fell asleep to the sounds of swoony brass choruses and whispered melodramatic dialogue.

The shopkeepers at Vanderbolt Furs changed the window display every Thursday. Thursdays were like holidays for Mrs. Steinmetz.

Hypnotized by a velvety knee-length model, she didn't see the black sedan pull to a stop behind her in the street, didn't hear its wide tires crunch the snow piled up by the curb. The man sitting in the back of the car rolled his window down. The end of his cigar glowed red in the winter evening.

Mrs. Steinmetz was rather plain, but she had lovely

skin, and her cheap, shabby clothes only did so much to conceal her voluptuous figure. An opera house full of fur-wrapped society matrons would've envied a balcony of her size.

Despite years of rapt window-gazing, Mrs. Steinmetz had never dared to enter Vanderbolt's emporium of dreams. Her creamy white flesh had never known the touch of mink.

"Excuse me please, Miss," the man in the back of the hulking automobile said. "I'd like a word with you."

Mrs. Steinmetz snapped out of her fur-lined reverie and shivered. She hugged her thin coat tightly around her, hunching her shoulders as she approached the car and the stranger inside it.

"Do you need directions, sir?"

"Pardon my indiscretion, dear Miss, but I noticed how you admire the mink coats offered for sale in that shop. Would you like to have one of them?"

Mrs. Steinmetz nearly fainted. This was only partly due to the cold, her soupy diet and post-shift fatigue. She thought her prayers were finally about to be answered by the Mink Fairy.

"Oh, yes. Oh, thank you, kind sir."

"Perhaps this can be arranged," the rich man said. "Get in. We'll take a jaunt uptown."

The spacious cab was warm and smelled pleasantly of rich tobacco. The chauffeur up front was dressed in the finest livery. The man beside her wore three-piece suit. The studs on his coat glittered like diamonds, which they were.

"Take us uptown, Jim," he said. "All the way."

The big car took off without a lurch, barely a sound. The driver seemed to have the traffic lights under his command. They all turned green to let them shush by.

"Would you care for a cocktail, Miss? I'm afraid I can only offer you rum, but it's damn fine rum."

"Oh yes please, sir. Thank you. I'd love a shot."

The decanter sparkled like an outscale jewel, as did the glass in which the rich man poured the dark liquor.

"Won't you please take off your wrap? You'll be so much more comfortable. Allow me to help you."

Mrs. Steinmetz blushed. She wasn't wearing her bra. She'd busted a strap that morning and hadn't had time to make the repair. The other girls at the factory didn't notice or care, and they all wore smocks anyway. Mrs. Steinmetz's smock was on its peg in the factory's workroom, and a rich stranger was about to help her out of her coat. She nearly flopped out the front of her calico dress when she leaned forward to accommodate him. Her nipples were still rock-hard from the cold.

"Oh my God," the rich man said. "I mean, excuse me, Miss, but you have such a marvelous bosom."

Mrs. Steinmetz attempted to cover herself. "Uhm, thank you, sir. Where we going? I thought..."

The wide, brightly lit avenues had given way to dark,

pitted streets. The skyscrapers had been replaced by shabby buildings with boarded-up windows. Even the snowdrifts looked black and menacing. Mrs. Steinmetz had never been so far uptown before.

A group of men stood outside a storefront whose red neon sign throbbed LIQUOR, with the U burnt out. The driver slowed as they passed. Black faces at them turned to glower.

"Keep going," the rich man instructed.

He poured himself another glass of rum. He poured Mrs. Steinmetz another glassful too, even though she initially tried to refuse. Her head was already swimming. She'd only eaten a few crackers and an apple that day for lunch.

A large black man walked slowly beneath the only streetlight still in function on a long block of vacant lots. He pushed along a wheelbarrow from which several wooden handles stuck out.

"Sweet sweating Christ, look at the shoulders on him. Stop, Jim."

The car rolled smoothly to a halt. The rich man leaned across Mrs. Steinmetz to roll down the window, spilling rum in her lap as he did so.

"Hey, big fella. Get over here a minute. I wanna talk to you."

The giant set down his wheelbarrow, wiped his hands on his jacket. His voice came in a low and deep.

"Whatchoo want?"

"Ever seen one of these, big boy?" The rich man

snapped a crisp $100 bill between his fingers. "All for you."

"How many I got to kill?"

"Nothing like that. All you gotta do is have some fun with this pretty lady here."

"But I got my tools here. I can't just…"

"No one around here wants them. Get in."

There was barely room in the back seat, though it had seemed broad as a football field moments before. Suddenly Mrs. Steinmetz felt dangerously crowded. The man smelled of dirt and sweat. They drove past a ruined church, a ghostly abandoned schoolyard.

"Whip it out," the rich man finally said.

"'Scuse me, sir?"

"You heard me, boy."

He sighed and began fumbling with his pants. Mrs. Steinmetz gasped when she saw what he was packing down there.

"Now," the rich man said, regarding her with a cold, merciless stare. "Get to work."

Mrs. Steinmetz felt like crying.

"Shut up," the rich man said. "You want that mink coat, don't you?"

"It's not that," she said. "I'm afraid he'll kill me with that thing."

"You've got the wrong idea, girly," the rich man said, narrowing his eyes at her bosom.

Mrs. Steinmetz understood. Nodding her head, she

slid down and knelt before the black giant between them, pulling down the top of her dress.

"You Jew-girls have a natural talent," the rich man said as she put her breasts to good use.

"Miss," the black man whimpered a minute, "you gonna make me..."

"Yes, oh yesss..." the rich man hissed.

He threw his head back and laughed as the car filled with moans of horrible delight.

Outside the nearest subway entrance, Jim handed Mrs. Steinmetz a new mink coat wrapped in plastic, fresh from the cleaners.

That fur still hangs in Mrs. Steinmetz's closet. She never wore it once.

Welcome to Felchville

A small party was on its way to a wedding in the country. Their budget rental car would've been more comfortable with one less person in it. Pete, in order to deserve his spot in back, kept up the conversation. A Hollywood hopeful, he lived in a Limbo of awaited phone calls, letters, any hint that the time had come to get out of New York and head west.

The Big City, Pete said, was finished. The theater was dead, newspapers were written by lickspittles, magazines were staffed by corrupt cliques, publishing companies were cabals run by Freemasons. There are a million Petes in town. He'd kept his sense of humor about it, though.

People had once said, you ought to be a professional comedian. Pete had worn out his welcome at the improv clubs. He wasn't on-stage funny. His laughs were on paper instead.

His embryonic screenplay was a box-office smashterpiece in search of a big idea. The evil twin thing, he said. The Great White Shark with the disco soundtrack: there's a little of him in everyone.

Wade Hawkes was at the wheel. His name was perfect for a director of Westerns, or a sheriff in a movie. Aside from being overweight, he looked the part. He taught film history at Columbia University.

Wade's wife Mona rode shotgun. She kept her eyes on the road. Wade didn't drive much, and was therefore clumsily aggressive. She was nervous.

Pete had wedged himself between Allie and me in back. Allie and I had been together a long time. She might've wanted to make it legal, at some point.

Edgar Whittemore, the man about to be married Upstate, was a lawyer. Despite his respectable position, he had found himself smushed up against a window.

Car dealerships and fast food oases gave way to farms, pastures, and forests. There wasn't much traffic in either direction.

"Can we please get off the highway?" Allie finally said. "I'd like to see some trees."

Wade swerved into the next exit, and the world outside went green, red, orange, yellow and brown.

Allie, an interior designer, was delighted when we drove past a Charles Addams-style mansion that'd recently been featured in one of her favorite magazines. "Ooh look! That's Sere Pines, the Suckley estate."

"Suck-lee," Pete drawled.

"Miss Suckley's like a modern Miss Havisham," Allie said, "in that she's not modern at all. She's a kooky old Yankee blueblood who keeps the family spread exactly the way it was in her Great-grandpa's day. Or maybe she let it rot away to honor his memory, or because she's got no money left. The Suckleys were the last of the New England loyalists."

"Omigod, look!" Pete squealed, nearly leaping into the front seat. "There's a sign up ahead! We're coming into Felchville."

He was right: the blue sign read FELCHVILLE. I'd never heard of the place. Maybe it didn't exist before we showed up.

Wade and Mona were both nonplussed. Felch wasn't part of their prenuptial agreement, nor of their general vocabularies.

Allie just groaned for her part. Among the accumulations in our cramped Times Square studio apartment was a vast collection of Underground Comix that will go to the Public Library when I die.

"Slow down, Wade," Pete said, grabbing the driver's shoulder. "I don't want to miss any of the details..."

Outwardly, Felchville seemed an ordinary drive-by burg, with all the usual shops, restaurants, parking lots and houses. Normally dressed normal-looking people wandered about their lives on clean, uncrumbled sidewalks.

"Ooh look!" Allie gasped, to humor Pete. "They all got brown crusts around their mouths..."

"They're just foaming," Pete spat in reply.

Felcher was a surname Allie and I had both seen on grave markers in Queens, and in parts of New Jersey as well. Cemetery expeditions were something to do on weekends, after we'd checked out the 6th Avenue flea market. There must be a million couples like us in town.

A man in a brown derby hat stopped to admire the local smoke-shop window, or perhaps his reflection in it. He looked repressed.

"Felch-a-holics Anonymous member," Pete said, with the accent on member.

"Why're they flying Canadian flags all over the place?" Allie said. "Did we mass-sleepwalk through the part where the Mounties waved us across the border?"

"November 12th is Canada Appreciation Day, here in Felchville," Pete said. "They celebrate by felching each other unconscious." He provided slurpy sound effects to accentuate his point.

Felchville had a public library. The red maple leaf banner on the thick pole that protruded from its facade flapped with civic pride.

There was a long line at the Felchville Cafe's takeout window.

"Find a spot, please," Pete said. "I need to investigate deeper..."

Wade parked the car and we got out. Mona stretched her arms above her head while Allie leaned against the car, cleaning her glasses on her shirt for a clearer look around.

As we made our way inside the dark brown building, we marveled at the all-brown decor of its interior. From the booths to the floor tiles to the rubberized lunch counter, nearly everything had been cast in some shade of brown.

Our waitress seemed to have a slight mustache problem, but closer inspection revealed foamy brown crusts at the corners of her mouth. Pete elbowed my ribs.

The waitress' nameplate read FELICIA. Pete didn't miss a beat.

"What's the Brown Plate Special today, Felcha?" he asked.

Felicia didn't bat an eyelash in response. "Cream of meatloaf," she replied.

"Oh, delicious. Who've you got cooking in there?" Pete asked, nodding toward the brown swinging double-doors to the kitchen.

"Huh? Oh, it's old Homer Suckley, same as always on Thursdays." She beat a ballpoint tattoo on her notepad. "So, how many Brown Plates? Awful good. Had some for breakfast, myself."

"Just plain oatmeal for me," Mona said.

But Pete just couldn't let go of anything that smacked of Felchville-abilia.

"Suckley, huh?" he asked. "Is he by chance related to the Suckley Mansion, visible from the road on the way up from the city? What's that place called, Allie?"

"You mean Sere Pines," Allie said.

"Looks like the haunted house in a baroque carnival. Inhabited by some crazy old rich lady..."

"That's a different Suckley family," Felicia said. "Suckley's a fairly common name around these parts, after all."

Wade broke in. "I'd like a Western omelette, please."

The waitress looked at Allie.

"Just a cup of coffee for me," she said.

"Would you like cream in it?"

"No thanks. Black."

"You mean, brown," Felicia the Felchville waitress said. "The coffee's brown, here."

"Oh. In that case, I'll have a glass of orange juice. Orange is just orange here, right?"

"Of course it is."

"You got fresh-squeezed?"

"You mean, fresh-sucked. We got a machine that sucks out the juice."

"How 'bout we cancel our orders and get outta here?" Allie said.

"Not so fast," Pete said. He made it sound as though Felchville were a byzantine practical joke, and that everyone was in on it except Allie. "I'll simply die if I don't try the Felchville Brown Plate Special."

"Me too," I said. "And may I please have some maple syrup with it?"

"Comes with maple syrup," Felicia said.

"Naturally," Pete said.

Meanwhile, he'd been eyeing an item on the far end of the counter: a clear plastic doughnut display with a bell-cover. He went over to inspect the thing, excitedly waving for us to follow.

"You gotta check this out!"

Doughnuts at the Felchville Cafe had creases down the middle. Their holes brimmed over with chocolate mousse.

"Oh my God," Pete gasped. "They look so scrumptious..."

The calligraphy on a folded slip of paper read, "Home-Made by Mrs. Annie Hainell. Help Your Self. 35¢." Adjacent to the pastry holder was a short stack of paper plates and sanitary tongs. Pete helped himself to a felch doughnut, dropping coins into the paper cup provided.

"Let's begone." I said, tossing a $20 bill onto the counter. "Screw the food. I got a feeling we shouldn't eat anything here anyway."

Meanwhile, Pete was already frenching the hole of his doughnut. "What the hell are you talking about? We can't leave. This place is a dream. The screenplay practically writes itself."

Mona and Allie both stood up. Wade, who looked hungry and might otherwise have been persuaded to stay, checked his watch.

"Let's ride," he said. "Ceremony's supposed to start at three, and we've still got fifty or sixty miles to go. We don't want be late, it's rude."

"Screw the wedding," Pete said. Chocolate foamed at the corners of his mouth. "In fact, fuck all primitive superstitious meaningless rituals."

"The deal was, we'd stop and just to have a look

around," Allie said. "We've seen enough, for my tastes. Curiosity satisfied."

"Felchville, adiós," Mona said as she led the group toward the exit. Wade jingled his car keys behind her.

"C'mon Pete," I said. "We can stop here again on the way back to town. We'll book a suite at the Felchville Hotel if you want."

"You're just humoring me," he said, and it was true. We'd planned to turn the rest of the wedding weekend into a cultural excursion: Saratoga Springs, Fort Ticonderoga, the Mohawk Trail.

"Just when I've found the place," he continued. "You don't want me to write a hit screenplay. You want me to fail, don't you? You want me to remain a loser, eternally stuck in New York. Don't you even want to find out what cream of meatloaf tastes like?"

"Not really," I said.

It was then that Felicia emerged from the kitchen, arm laden with steaming brown porcelain plates.

"Bon appetit," Mona said unconvincingly.

Pete wolfed the rest of his doughnut and sat down resolutely at the counter. "So long, suckers," he said. "You can come visit me in Hollywood when my work here is finished."

Out on the street, a Felchville cop in a brown uniform was writing out a ticket. Wade, distracted by Felchville scenery, apparently hadn't noticed the Sanitation Dept Only sign.

"Sorry 'bout that, Officer," Wade said.

"There's a special cell for scofflaws in the Felchville Jail," the cop replied.

Or something like that.

Wade took the summons and we slowly drove away.

We arrived at the wedding late, missing the part of the ceremony where they say they do and they will.

At the banquet hall, the bride asked where Pete was. She was one of his ex-girlfriends, I guess I forgot to mention that. Actually, she was one of my ex-girlfriends too. From high school.

"He's in Heaven," I said.

Her eyes bulged in disbelief. She would've burst out crying, but didn't want to wreck her makeup.

"Sorry," I reassured her. "I meant, he's in a good place."

"Hollywood?"

"Yeah, Hollywood. He finally figured out how to get there."

"I knew he'd be okay in the end," she said. "I always thought he'd make it, eventually. I just didn't have enough patience to wait around for all his dreams to come true."

And with that, she disappeared back into the wedding whirl, to greet her other guests and dance with her new husband. I asked Allie to dance with me, and she agreed.

Zoo Tail

Her ass said, follow me. The way she walked, loosely translated from body language, said, look at my ass. The message was: look at my ass and follow me.

She headed towards the zoo.

This seemed an oddball destination for a woman dressed to hook. Hook up, I mean. Maybe with a friendly guy who doesn't spend sunny afternoons in an office or shop. She spotted the tail immediately. I'm no private detective. She didn't make a fuss or call the cops. She looked back to make sure I was still there behind her.

The zoo's a good place to go because it's free. Zoo management did some market research, and discovered the admission charge discouraged attendance. The free zoo became a popular attraction. Zookeepers made up for lost ticket sales with a popcorn stand. People stand in line to buy paper boxes of cloud-shaped kernels to feed the monkeys.

The lady with the wonderful behind sashayed through the wrought-iron gate. A zookeeper in a cop-like uniform said a big hello.

She was apparently a regular, well-known to the keepers and the sweepers who follow the elephants around. She's on a first-name basis with the giraffes, zebras, warthogs and giant anteaters.

A hand-painted sign said, Monkey Island. A green arrow pointed left. She stopped and pretended to study the sign. She looked back.

Modern life means less and less contact with animals. Less genuine contact with other people too, even though we're smashed closer and closer together, all the time, more and more of us every day. But those of us not confined to office space-and-time are free to go outside for fresh air, sunshine and a glimpse of caged nature. I hadn't been to the zoo in ages.

Monkey Island isn't a natural geographical phenomenon. Zoo architects dreamed up concrete poured into the shape of a tropical paradise. Just like the ones the general public saw on television while they were growing up, except no palm trees, no beach. Monkey Island is an island only because of its gray, garbage-strewn moat. People throw popcorn at the monkeys. Monkeys love popcorn. They wolf down as much popcorn as they can get their mitts on. But some popcorn inevitably ends up in the listless sludge that surrounds their artificial habitat. Kids in particular are not such amazing popcorn-tossers.

The woman didn't stop at the popcorn stand. Either she had no dough to blow on frivolous fripperies like feeding monkeys, or else she thought it cruel to make imprisoned creatures turn somersaults for insubstantial snacks. She went to the wrought-iron railing that surrounds the water that surrounds Monkey Island and separates visitors from the resident apes, and leaned over.

Her rear curves were accentuated by how far she

leaned. Man oh man those lucky monkeys got one hell of a cleavage peep.

Perfecto. Time to sidle up, lean casually against the fence and say, "'Scuse me, Miss, but these monkeys sure are fascinating creatures. Sometimes when I watch monkeys I can't help but think maybe them and us aren't so different after all. Except the poor monkeys are stuck in a cage and we, for the time being at least, are pretty much free to move around and do as we please."

Then, if fate will have it, a pair of baboons will start humping. She'll get the idea. Carnal blossoms will expand and unfold. In one of our formerly lonely bedrooms, or in a public toilet stall at the zoo.

She swayed back and forth against the railing, teetered on the brink between the world of people, captive ape territory and dirty water. The watery barrier reflected an upside-down face, a bosom about to spill from a clingy blouse and clouds. On the opposite shore, a pink-ass macaque daintily drank and shot a monkey moon at another monkey with a hard-on.

He was the biggest ape on Monkey Island, some kind of monster gorilla or mandrill, and he was looking at my lady.

He wasn't exactly handsome, not even for an orangutan. Looked like the zoo barber had taken a defective razor to his pelt. His fur was thin, clumpy, tufted, in patches. He either suffered from simian skin disease, ape-zema, or else stir-craziness had gone psychosomatic on his all-over ape hairdo.

My fantasy girlfriend wasn't offended by the balding animal's behavior. Neither was she amused. Most people would go hurh-hurh check it out the freaky chimp's pullin' his banana. Then they'd wander off to gawk at the demon-faced hyena. My lady stayed put, bent over, waved her caboose like a cat, and stared.

The colossal howler monkey or lemur or whatever he was stared right back at the lady who was watching him beat his meat. No way to tell if he was just feeling good because the sun was shining warm and pleasant, or if he was excited because she showed up and leaned over. A feeling hit that this was a regular thing for the lady and the monkey. They were engaged in the only kind of date they could legally have, but someone had intruded on their illusion of privacy.

So I didn't try to start up a conversation with her. Maybe I should've. She might've snapped out of her trance and come along for some human-to-human intercourse. Or she might've told me to get lost and that would've been the end.

Another feeling took over. This was something secret, forbidden, hot. The monkey component of my brain said, expose yourself and behave like the confined primate. But you can get locked up for indecent acts in public. There are kids at the zoo, most days. Kids shouldn't have to see stuff like that.

Field day giggles galore arise from kids who watching a chimp slam the ham.

Incidentally, Ham was the name of the first chimp to be blasted off into outer space. Black and white newspaper pix of a monkey in a space suit. He gave a toothy grin for the camera, but man did his eyes ever look sad.

Teacher, teacher, what's the monkey doing? More snickers as the embarrassed schoolmarm hustles the punks along to gawp at the rhinoceros. The rhino takes a gushing leak on his bed of straw. Shit-eating scavenger birds scatter and fly away because they're free.

If the lady had noticed that a stranger stared, she gave no sign of it. The chimp shot an annoyed smirk, or as close as a monkey's mug can get to one, and yanked harder. Then he stopped. Watery semen spurted and splatted on cement. Another caged creature, perhaps a female baboon, ambled over on all fours, stuck a finger into the milky puddle, sniffed, tasted, shuffled away to snuffle up a kernel of popcorn someone who hadn't stopped to watch the monkey show had thrown.

The lady stared at the gorilla or orangutan or whatever it was and squirmed her hips. The monkey kept his eye on me. There, is that what you wanted to see? Will that do, for today?

It won the staring contest, hands down. When I looked over, the lady was gone. She'd walked away and I missed her part of the show.

At least there was no admission charge.

The guy in charge of the zoo's popcorn concession didn't even look up when I paid for the smallest cardboard box of popcorn on offer. Big deal, another cheapo customer. First thing you learn in the Big City is don't make eye contact. He played by the rules.

Zoo etiquette is you feed the monkeys one fluffy kernel at a time. Bond with a lower form of life. Feed the monkeys as though you were their lord and master. Make urbane comments on their antics. Instead, I winged the box at the jack-off monkey's head. Either I missed or he ducked like lightning. Popcorn exploded all over a section of Monkey Island's cement floor and started a furry feeding frenzy. The spent ape folded his arms over a patch of leathery chest and closed his black eyelids. For him, the rest of the world was gone.

It's possible the sexy lady went back to the zoo the next day for another date with her monkey. True-life stories abound about desirable women who fix their love and souls on prison lifers, Death Row losers. They waste their lives in trailers parked just outside prison grounds. They live for full-contact visiting hours.

No more zoo trips for me.

But I learned something. The difference between monkeys and apes is that apes don't have tails. I don't have a tail. So maybe I'm an ape. An ape who tails weirdoes, unless they're headed to the zoo.

A Letter to the Editor

My co-worker Francine (not her real name) always sent so many mixed signals.

Though a confirmed metrosexual, I consider myself straight. I try to dress well, work out, use hair- and skin-care products. Many women at work pay compliments, but Francine went further. She winked, sometimes even "copped a feel" of my suits and ties. She asked for fashion tips, and we used to go on lunch-hour shopping safaris together.

Francine's older than I am. She's married, but that wouldn't stop some guys I know.

When Francine said, "Let's meet in Conference Room A", which was unoccupied at the time, I thought we were about to cross a line.

Well, we did, but the line we crossed was unexpected to say the least.

She whispered that the Boss had asked to see her in his office, and she needed to be sure she looked "correct". Be brutal, she said, like on TV. Disappointed, I said she looked fine.

She hiked her skirt, unbuttoned her blouse.

"Think this is too much?"

Maybe I shook my head.

She pulled off her shoes. "Do my feet smell?"

She sat on the conference table, raised her legs, and put her feet in my face. I said they smelled fine.

She gave me a peck on the cheek.

"Thanks," she said. Wait for me after work."

She went off to face The Boss. I stayed in the Conference Room to cool down. This took a while.

The thing is, Francine's feet *did* smell.

The rest of the workday was a total loss.

Francine waltzed into my cubicle after the whistle blew.

"It worked!" she said. "I made vice-president. Thanks for giving me the confidence. Let's have a drink to celebrate. My treat."

At the bar, Francine put her hand on my knee, practically licked my ear as she spoke into it, and gave what I thought were several significant looks.

After a few martinis, I finally blurted out, "Why don't we go to a room or something?"

She looked at me as though I'd just vomited.

"With you? But you're a..."

Instead of correcting her in that moment, for some reason I thought it better to confess what had gotten me so hot about her in the first place.

"Oh my god that's so disgusting," she said. "And now I gotta worry about foot odor on top of it..."

All I could do was pray that the stuffed shark hanging above our booth would fall on my head and kill me right then and there.

Francine said she wouldn't pay for drinks after all. Instead, she was going to tell her husband what I'd said to her. He's a pro wrestler or a bodyguard or something like that.

At least he won't send mixed signals.

Take It Off and Say Goodbye

Derek's girlfriend Yvonne was a stripper. She danced two nights a week at Joe Rae's, on 6th Avenue and 24th Street. Joe Rae took one look and gave her Fridays and Saturdays on the spot. She also danced out in Queens, and at another place in Jersey City. She kept her tits and ass busy.

Derek and I worked together, but we weren't bankers or lawyers or doctors or anything. We were editors at a weekly sex newspaper.

Derek was of medium height, skinny, always dressed in black. He wore near-opaque sunglasses, even at night. There used to be a million guys like him in New York. I always thought Yvonne should've been involved with someone more interesting. Like me, for instance.

Yvonne's hair was like neatly stacked marine rope. She was from Illinois and had a bit of a heroin habit. She'd nod off at odd times and there always seemed to be a slight, constant trickle from her upturned nose, but it didn't seem like anything to go into rehab about.

As the sex newspaper's Art Director, my job was to look at pussy all day long. That wasn't enough, however, and so I went to Joe Rae's topless bar nearly every night as well. There's a big difference between pictures and the real thing, even if all you get to do is look. Though it wasn't strictly legal, Joe Rae's girls would pull aside their G-strings for a dollar. If they'd seen you around, or if they liked your face, they'd work some finger-magic, too. Some nights, a low-tide tang clung to my beard like fog.

Pussy's nice to look at. I guess I like looking at it more than dealing with it. But it wasn't just pussy that kept me coming back to Joe Rae's. I really loved his place.

Joe Rae was an old hippie, even older than me. He stuffed the jukebox with Cream, Hendrix and the Stones. Some of the dancers complained there was no disco or Latin. Joe gave them quarters and bills to feed the glowing slot, and strippers became adolescent girls in a department store who'd been told they could have all the makeup they wanted for free.

Drinks at Joe Rae's cost the same as at normal dives. The girls never asked, but you could buy them a drink and they'd sit with you and chat for a while.

The decor at Joe Rae's hadn't changed since it'd been an Italian social club. The red flocked wallpaper was sticky to the touch and hung with amateurish oils of Palermo and Naples. There was also an old picture of a young man who'd been killed in Korea.

That hand-tinted black-and-white photo bothered me sometimes: a guy in uniform, with a toothy smile and sad eyes, all geared up to kill commies overseas. They killed him instead. Born in New York, 1930, died at Inchon, 1952, Corporal Joseph DeRamo might've been tickled from beyond the grave that his shrine was in a topless bar. It always seemed kind of strange that Ma and Pa DeRamo hadn't taken their boy's picture with them when they finally closed up shop. Maybe they'd left just as abruptly, for that place where you can't bring anything along. I asked Joe Rae, but he didn't know his place's history. The rolling metal shutters had been down a long time when he'd finally bought it.

Bikers sold crank at the Teddy Bare. Boob-job skells hustled ginger ale champagne at the Pla-Z-Boy. It cost ten bucks just to get past the threadbare velvet rope at Limoncello's. Joe Rae's had no such drawbacks. I never got diarrhea from the free-buffet meatballs. The men's restroom wasn't a gay pick-up scene, not that there's anything wrong with that. Even the bouncers acted friendly.

Not all of Joe Rae's women were as beautiful as Yvonne, but some of them were real dancers, and it was nice to be there just to watch them move. A Canadian amazon who could touch the back of her head with the soles of her feet stayed in town long enough to get me obsessed. I handed over ten-dollar bills until one night she was gone.

There were junkie girls, and ladies who looked like they'd carve you up with a razor for whatever was in your pocket.

Joe Rae even gave bigger women a chance. Baby Blue looked like she'd been carved from a block of cellulite, but she was a crowd-pleaser nonetheless. She shimmied hard for her finale. Cottage cheese crammed into flesh-colored pantyhose vibrated and shook while the sweat sprayed. She was powdered with stardust, but I never asked how she got home, or where that home might be.

Yvonne told Joe Rae she didn't want to strip any more. She'd decided she wanted to get into the music business.

The founder and publisher of the sex newspaper heard of Yvonne's career dreams through her boyfriend, Derek. Our boss had a soft spot for his employees' girlfriends, especially the ones who may or may not have blown him for a hundred bucks in the stairwell at one of the XXX-mas parties he threw every year, attendance mandatory. The big man said Yvonne must have a farewell party at Joe Rae's, and that he would sponsor the event.

The editorial offices of the sex newspaper were on 14th Street. They occupied a high floor with sweeping views of midtown Manhattan. The walls were covered with obscene graffiti left by contributing cartoonists and illustrators.

My office was next to Derek's. We spoke to each other through open doors, but not that often. Since he had a year or two of college English under his belt, he turned our illiterate employer's ramblings into sentences and paragraphs. He drew from readers' deliria and edited stories from outside writers on an Army Surplus electric typewriter. Derek had created the publication's voice.

The paper's scumbag look was my baby. I dropped out of Art School. The black-and-white pictures came from inexhaustible battleship-gray file cabinets.

Our boss ran the operation with his own money. He was the one who went to prison when The Man said he must, which was often.

A few women worked at the sex weekly. Miss Gloria was the boss' long-suffering personal assistant. A slightly addled Jewish lady handled accounting and advertising. Long tall Cindy did the cut-and-paste layouts. She was from Florida.

The entire staff was practically ordered to attend Miss Yvonne's Farewell to the Stripper Life party.

The affair started at nine. Everyone went home to change into festive attire. In my case, a basement dump in Brooklyn and the last shirt left with a collar, which had grown tight since I'd last worn it.

The underground scene was represented by a grizzled poet and a director of nudie art films. Vinnie the Bouncer stood at the door and told the businessmen and college guys, "Sorry, we got a private event tonight. Joe Rae'll buy you a beer next time."

What went on at Yvonne's goodbye party was the same as what went on any other night, except the drinks were all free. Felt like in a dream I had, a nightmare, I guess, in which New York City was Hell. The only things different were that the subway was free and there was no Statue of Liberty in the burning harbor.

At midnight, Yvonne would do her last show. Then, like a princess in a fairy tale, she'd disappear and keep her clothes on forever after.

We ripped into the spread, catered by the boss'

favorite deli. Free liquor made things jollier. Cindy the Paste-up Girl, who'd held onto her Florida accent, talked about how she used to hit Plato's Cave every weekend, before Town Hall shut the place down.

She seemed wistful, as though the swinger scene had been some glorious chapter in human history.

There were so many women like her in town, loose and slightly nuts. They can't all own art galleries or run ad agencies. New York was a Hell for dashed female aspirations.

Yvonne emerged from the toilet. The other girls onstage applauded and lingered briefly to fondle her. Hendrix played "Little Wing" from the jukebox.

Hendrix was dead. So many evenings I'd sat there thinking that this was what it was all about, in the end. Joy and rage and thinking things could be different boiled down to thighs spread for a dollar.

Yvonne went all the way. Her G-string flew. Decency laws exploded. She backed up against the mirror wall streaked with femme-grease, spread her legs and sank down slow.

Goodbye to being young. Goodbye to whatever it was that everyone thought was supposed to happen. Goodbye to the idea that dropping out could lead somewhere good. Goodbye to topless bars.

The music biz, in Yvonne's case, turned out to be selling used records at Bleecker Billy's.

There was a positive side to her career change, though. She met a skaggy guitar player and finally dumped Derek. At least I thought it was positive.

Yvonne's last move on that final night was a backwards bend-over. I didn't want to see her go. I couldn't have her. She wouldn't be mine. I asked, once.

Turned out I couldn't have Joe Rae's, either. The laws changed, and the place went through a brief bikini-dance phase, but not many guys will tip girls in bathing suits on the off-chance that a nipple will pop out. There's hornier stuff on television.

Joe Rae, unlike Yvonne, had no last hurrah. He didn't sell his business, he closed it. Or maybe he *tried* to sell the place. I heard he moved to Mexico.

The green awning out front said Joe Rae's Topless. Then for a while it said Joe Rae's STopless, with the S hand-painted on, not even stenciled. The wind tore the awning, and it flapped like a flag. It still said STopless, but it wasn't true.

A Pipe Dream

The sound of waves and roller coaster screams came in through the bathroom window in Niv's motel room: my favorite place in the world. I'd hose down my wetsuit and shake the Pacific chill in the shower, hang out in the steam to watch the sun go down and the fog roll in.

Niv lived at the Tramonto Motel with his Iranian girlfriend. Her family ran a Persian restaurant up in San Francisco. They disapproved of their daughter's lifestyle choices, but they still sent money anyway. Her brother rolled back and forth between the States and Tehran. He always had opium. The restaurant connection was a perfect cover. He shipped the dope in bottles of pomegranate syrup. He came down to Santa Cruz often, to visit his sister and get stoned with her and her friends.

His name rhymed with Ay-rab, so that's what I called him. He'd get all heated and sputter that Iranians weren't arabs, like anyone cared. I can't remember his sister's name, or if it rhymed with anything.

Ay-rab was nice to look at. He and his sister worked on their tans in minimal Euro-style beachwear while Niv and I caught waves. Back at the motel, she'd cook Iranian dinners and we'd blow opium. The motel was built to look like an ocean liner, with portholes for windows and fake smokestacks on the roof. The room smelled of poppy resin, and pomegranate syrup cooking down.

Big Dan dropped by with his sister Kath. She was new in town, fresh from a divorce or a less formal break-up with some black guy over in Stockton.

Kath was wearing one of her brother's sweatshirts, about four sizes too large. Her shorts made her thighs bulge when they didn't have to. Flowery flipflops showed off her blackened soles and chipped toenail polish. When she pulled down the hood it looked like someone had gone over her hair with bacon rinds. Smelled that way, too.

Motel room rhymes with womb and tomb. Kath squatted down to hit the pipe, and didn't even ask what was in it. An intimate whiff of herself blended in with opium smoke and Iranian grub. I stared, and got lost in a stoned dream of her soaping up in the shower not far away.

Big Dan shot me an ugly look. He was close to seven feet tall, weighed over two hundred pounds. He was the human hydraulic lift at a garage on the outskirts of town. He reamed out corroded pistons with his bare hands, or his hard cock. *Lay off my sister*, the look said. *She's in a bad place right now.*

Opium bugs crawled around like a family of cockroaches under my skin, which felt just like a wetsuit. Dreams rolled in like waves and mist from the ocean.

Niv changed records. His olive-skinned lady brought in dinner and we ate it on the floor.

Ay-rab seemed really interested in what Big Dan had to say about slant-six engine blocks. He opened his caramel-colored eyes wide, and wagged his head slightly off the beat from the speakers.

Kath rose shakily to go to the bathroom. She came back with a flush fanfare and dropped down again, slightly closer than she'd been before. I handed her the pipe. She showed a chipped front tooth when she smiled.

Niv's woman took her shirt off. Those two were real make-out artists.

Big Dan was explaining what *ring job* meant. Ay-rab scratched, nodded, blinked and mouthed *oh wow*. He packed more opium into the pipe with a little knife.

"You've got good hair," I told Kath. "But you don't treat it right. Look at you: no body, bounce or sheen."

She shrugged, scratched her crotch. She had sorrows to forget, pain to medicate. She put Zippo to pipe-hole and sucked in deep.

Looked like a movie flickering on a distant screen when I reached out to flick a limp strand. Kath said quit it, like we were back in fourth grade. So I flicked her again.

Then I must've nodded out. I was in a sideshow: The Man in the Chicken-Wire Cage Full of Snakes. My job was to sit there barely even breathing while cottonmouths, copperheads, fat rattlers and cobras crept and crawled all over me. Suckers in Sunday clothes paid a quarter for a look and a shiver. A Gaboon viper flicked his forked tongue, sensed a carotid artery nearby and lunged menacingly. But if I flinched one inch, all the other snakes would sink their fangs right in.

Kath's voice pulled me out of the snake-pit. "What *is* this stuff, anyway? Got me all sleepy..."

The only light was a beam from under the utility kitchen door and the stereo's green glow. Niv and his motel wife humped away to the drone music under a mound of sleeping bags, blankets and clothes on the motel bed. The heap rose and fell in the gloom. The springs creaked in tune with their gasps and moans.

Meanwhile, Ay-rab and Big Dan were off in Dreamland, transfixed by the live love show.

"Kath, let's face it: your hair's a mess. *You're* a mess. Let's hit the shower and see what we can do. Come on."

She tripped over her brother's legs. We bumped the bed. I locked the bathroom door. The dim bathroom light seemed surgical after the motel room's gloom. I unscrewed one of the lightbulbs over the mirror at the sink. Kath held her arms up like a kid so I could pull the dirty sweatshirt over her head. Her tits flopped out and bounced upon release. Cool air from the open window stiffened her nipples.

A black mamba went for my jugular vein.

Kath's shorts hit the floor. No panties. Female funk filled the air. I stripped like getting naked was no big deal, turned the knob, checked the temperature, pulled her into the stall.

Niv's woman had barrels of hair-care products

stockpiled in there. I moved Kath around like a doll, kept her nose and mouth out of the spray so she wouldn't drown. I became the hairdresser who'd make her look like the girl in the shampoo ad of her dreams.

Green gunk oozed from one of the bottles. I massaged it into her scalp. Gray foam formed, like roadside slush-monsters seen from bus windows back East. Rinse and repeat, apply conditioner and let it steam. Steam was fine, but smoke was better. I pulled Kath from the shower, sat her on the sink. "Don't move," I said.

A needle skated uselessly on black vinyl. Niv and his woman were still screwing like dogs. Ay-rab was sucking Big Dan's big dick. He was good at it. I almost stayed to watch, but grabbed the pipe and a lighter instead.

Kath had slumped forward on the sink.

She sucked the smoke hungrily.

"It's working," she whispered. "It's like I can feel my hair coming alive."

Like snakes. Medusa. Men turn to rock.

There was a chrome blowdryer on the shelf, and a pair of scissors.

A yellow butterfly tattoo on Kath's left shoulder showed in the clouded mirror. I hit the pipe and began to snip.

Kath took another big hit and pulled me into her face to shotgun the smoke. She had teeth missing. She squirmed, bucked her hips against me, moaned she needed love, bad.

But I had a haircut to finish. My ears filled with invisible music. My hands flew.

The mirror gradually cleared, showing the unholy mess I'd made of Kath's head.

Her cement-boned brother Big Dan was in the next room. Outside, mist rolled in off the Pacific. Waves roared in darkness. Sharks glided just below their surface.

Better re-fog the mirror. Steam billowed from the shower like a dream of incense-breathing dragons.

Kath, limp with romance, glamour and opium, let herself be dragged back into the stall.

"Let's get the stray hairs off you, or you'll be itchy all over."

New boys in the Marine Corps had better haircuts. Nothing left but the Final Solution, which in this case wasn't placenta-based conditioner.

Niv's woman kept a quiver of razors in the shower. Shampoo can be used as shave cream. Kath was too stoned to maintain erect posture. She sunk to a showerstall squat and did what came naturally.

A surf bum no longer, I became some kind of monk whose saffron robes flapped in sunlight and a stiff breeze that blew from snow-mountains in the background.

Kath was a monastic novice who still lived in the sensory world that was maya, illusion, vanity. She had to learn, pray, meditate. But first she had to get her monk look down. I shaved Kath's head to serve God's will.

Then I shaved my own, and took my left eyebrow off too.

Kath kept on doing what she did best. The drain was clogged with hair. Dirty water and human fluids rose, overflowed. Then the motel's hot water ran out.

Nude bald stoners shivered in a shower stall in Santa Cruz. We couldn't stay in there forever. We had to face what passes for reality, in this world.

When I unlocked the door, Niv's lady rushed in as though she was about to explode. She squealed when she saw the horror.

Niv was sprawled on the bed. Big Dan was nailing Ay-rab to the floor. He got a load of Kath.

"Whu'd you do to my sister, motherfucker? I'm gonna take you apart."

"Shut up, you big homo."

He stared, open-mouthed. He shut up.

Big Dan later beat up Ay-rab for turning him gay.

Kath liked her new hairdo, for a little while. We went to a wig shop just off the boardwalk and got a magenta Louise Brooks model from the bargain bin. She liked the wig even better.

Niv still lives in the ship-shaped motel, but he never invited us back.

Big Black Widow

Here she comes, stomping down Fifth Avenue, a sexual nightmare on two legs: Big Mary, the terror of all those smaller than her. In other words, everyone.

So many years since she last tore herself out of the shadows.

She was still horribly beautiful, and dressed in black.

Her black hat was hung with a black veil. Long black gloves showed off her biceps and the whiteness of her skin. At fifty paces, she had me on the verge of premature ejaculation.

She didn't see me, or *couldn't* see me. Lesser creatures, the ants all around her, don't really exist. We're just packets of energy with little or no mass, aimlessly adrift in nature, while she spans and dominates the world. I could've turned around, or ducked into a building, or grabbed a cab. She closed in, staring off into space. Her eyes blazed red, as though she'd been weeping.

"Hey Mary." We'd been off our playground across the Hudson River for decades, so I didn't say, Hey *Big* Mary. That old nickname might still have been a torment to her.

She looked around. She seemed lost. 'Maybe she doesn't live in the city,' I thought. 'She's just here for the day because someone she loved, or admired, has died.' It was still difficult to imagine that Big Mary could have friends. What a huge, lonely life she must've led.

"Oh. Hey. It's you." Her lips moved slowly, like the wings of some magnificent demon.

"Wow, you look exactly the same," I said. "I mean, you look great. How *are* you?"

Man how stupid can you be? You see a woman dressed in mourning, and ask her how she's doing.

"Oh, great, except that I'm a widow now."

"Oh no. I'm sorry. How long were you married?"

I mean, who the hell *was* the lucky guy? A professional wrestler? A monster from Hollywood? And how did you kill him?

"Not even twenty years," she said.

"Well hey, that's more than most couples get."

The more I spoke, the more I felt I hadn't grown or made any progress since the woman I'd just bumped into arrested my development in the Fifth Grade. But that was already more education than most people got.

"Yeah I guess," Big Mary said. "Hadn't thought of it that way, yet."

A moment was about to slip by. Had to grab it, get it back, make it stay, but moments are much more powerful than they seem. When they want to go, they go.

"So, uh, you live around here?"

The Upper East Side, where everyone who doesn't live there wants to, was her natural habitat.

"Yeah. It's weird, our apartment's in the same building as the funeral parlor. I mean, how convenient. You die, all you gotta do is head downstairs. Don't even have to put a sweater on."

It was early spring, a bright day with a cutting chill wind. Big Mary hugged herself with her formidable arms.

"Jeezus, maybe I *should've* put a sweater on. I got a whole goddamn closet full of cashmere and camel hair."

Herds of alpacas and vicuñas had been rendered into cloud-like garments to warm Big Mary's broad alabaster shoulders.

She looked at me, then. We were more or less eye-to-eye.

Memory plays tricks with perspective and creates monsters. Black clothes accentuate height. Big Mary used to wear drab monochrome outfits to school. They were custom-made by her Mom, since store-bought clothes were expensive, and none of the shops in town had anything that'd fit her colossal daughter anyway. Mary's family was poor.

She let me drape my coat across her shoulders. "Jeezus Mary, you used to scare the hell out of me. I used to have nightmares where you'd clomp down the street and knock down buildings and uproot trees. No matter where I hid, you'd find and eat me."

"Oh yeah?" She looked as though she'd forgotten her

husband's funeral for a moment. "Maybe fate has brought us together today so I could say I'm sorry."

So she remembered the time she and her ogress cronies dragged me into the little house-schwitz on the playground. They tied me up with a jump-rope and threw me to the floor. Big Mary loomed overhead, straddled me, and dropped to her knees. Torture was a kiss, something grade school boys were supposed to dread. But she also whispered that she was going to suck the eyeballs out of my head.

That was one long, dark recess.

"Tell me about you," Big Mary said. "You live in the city these days? Whuddya do?"

"Oh I write stories. For kids, mostly. Not little kids, though. Big kids, I guess."

"Yeah? You make a living at it?"

"Not really. Not anymore. You got kids?"

"Zero. You?"

"None for me too. I split up with my girlfriend a while back. We had twelve years together. That was all we got. Too bad, because I think we both wanted more."

"Well that's pretty funny, isn't it, us bumping into each other like this after so long and we're both sorta available. I mean, you *are* loose, aren't you?"

"Let's go for a walk in the park, Mary. There's a place I like."

"You haven't turned into some kinda ax-murderer, have you?"

"Oh, you never know."

"Okay, let's go. I don't mind."

She didn't say, 'I ain't afraid of you or anyone like you.' She'd grown polite over time, it seemed.

The place I liked was near the carousel. The roundabout was curtained off and closed, due to the wind and cold. A playground for ghosts, the spirits of children who grew up and weren't children anymore, though of course deep down inside they still were and would always be. The clearing was quiet and isolated.

Big Mary pulled a face. "You *like* this place? That's so weird, cuz it always gives me the creeps. I always jog around it so I don't have to look."

"You're in great shape. You look like a..." I was about to say, 'glamorous bodyguard'. "...a dancer, some kinda full-contact ballerina."

"I just try to keep from falling all the way apart is all." That New Jersey accent won't go away ever, I thought.

The carousel dissolved in the raking light. The city beyond the trees had dematerialized. I led Big Mary into a stand of ironwoods that grew from the mouth of a red brickwork tunnel. She said, "Look, I already apologized for what I did. I wasn't really gonna hurt you anyway. I only wanted to smooch-rape you cuz I thought you were cute. Honest."

"This is known as psycho-drama, Mary. It's supposed to help people get over past traumas."

"Okay, go ahead and kill me if you want. Do it quick,

though. I'm not into pain."

"You got the wrong idea. We bring the past back to life in order to make it go away."

I was lying. I lay down on the dirt, face up. The carousel's organ began to play. The wind wheezed a ghostly music through its pipes.

"What the hell are you doing?"

The wind blew Big Mary's veil off her face. The lines showed. The years pounced into the moment like hyenas.

"This is the only playground we got left, Mary. Do it. But go all the way this time. Please."

"You don't mean it," she said, but she knew I did.

She moved, towered over the visible world, the way she had back at school. Her black skirt was a shroud, her black lace panties a chic touch of death. She went down slow, put pressure where the air went in, and where the blood raced to the brain. She knew what to do, where to go, how to meet a millionaire husband and how to snuff him when the time was right. Oh you big gorgeous cunning killer.

Everything was so sweet and black and final. But then she stopped, stood up, and let the light have its way again. Sometimes I hate light.

"Why not, Mary?" I gasped. "Back then you said forever and ever."

"We were in Fifth Grade, for chrissakes."

"Life used to be so scary and serious," I said. "Then it got light and sorta fun for a while, and now it's all so dumb and meaningless."

"Nothing changes," she said. "The only thing that's different is that when you're all grown up it's okay to be the biggest thing around."

She straightened her stockings, her skirt, set her veil back where it belonged.

"What're you doing this evening?" I brushed myself off, shook the dead leaves and grass out of my hair. "Do you have to go to some gargantuan funeral banquet, or can I take you out on a date?"

"That's what I wanted you to ask me out there on the playground," she said.

We went to the Stork Club for drinks, had dinner at Delmonico's, danced at Studio 54 and wound up as close to the stars as possible, at Windows on the World. The harbor and New Jersey sparkled like crazy below. We watched a storm come in off the Atlantic to erase the night and shake the skyscrapers to their foundations.

The next morning we went to the old Penn Station, that Roman Temple dedicated to Cronos, and caught a train to Jersey City to visit our old school. But the old red building had been torn down. An octoplex cinema was there instead, and its parking lot had engulfed the playground.

The Swinging Bikers

Geezer wanted my wife, I wanted his. So there was no problem, except our wives weren't interested.

Wait, that came out wrong. Our wives were interested in sex, but not swapping.

They didn't give any reasons when we asked why not.

We routinely got nude and had sex in front of each other. We even got married together. But whenever we suggested mixing things up a bit, the ladies acted like we'd hurt their feelings.

Geezer and I discussed the situation at Mother's, a roadhouse.

"We either find some new old ladies," I said. "Or sneak out with some looser ones."

"Forget that. Lurleen once saw me glance at another woman, and I didn't care for the look in her eye. Foolin' around leads to lawyers, and lawyers lead to the loss of our hogs in the divorce battle. We have to convince the girls that swapping's cool."

"How?"

"Maybe I have the answer."

"Far out. What is it?"

"DMT."

"C'mon. That's like vitamin D, for those two."

"The Satan's Scamps bro who sold it to me said it's special stuff. He *did* mention there might possibly be side-effects."

"We'll worry about side-effects afterwards."

***

Next evening, we rode up Crested Skull Hill. We entered the cave that made the left eye-socket and threw down our stuff.

A full moon shone on spent condoms, empty bottles and roaches from parties past.

"Big treat tonight," Geezer said, as he smoothed out an old blanket on the cave floor.

"Whatcha talkin' about, Geezer?" My wife Babette sounded suspicious.

"It's uh, hard to explain." he said.

Lurleen, Geezer's wife, said, firmly, "No needles."

"Calm down," Geezer said. "This is a special occasion."

"Oh yeah?" Babette sounded even more suspicious. "What special occasion is that?"

"The anniversary of when I realized Lurleen was the only one for me."

"Is that true, honey?" Moonlight glinted off a tear in Lurleen's eye.

"Naturally, my love."

"Aw, ain't that sweet," Babette said, unconvincingly.

The pop of beer bottles seemd to reassure her. Clink, clank, clunk, we drunk to true love, and then the ladies took their pills.

Geezer and I must've stared.

"Hey! What's going on?" Babette said. "How come you guys aren't…"

The stuff kicked in fast. Babette licked her chops and lunged for Geezer. He giggled as my wife tore down his pants.

Lurleen fell to her knees. I felt like crying.

Life was different. The world had changed. Heaven was real.

Spent, I hugged Lurleen tight. "That was great," I said.

"You aren't done yet, clown."

"Huh?"

"I need more." Her voice was deep, hoarse. Purple searchlights shot from her eyes.

"Gimme a minute to recover. Let's smoke a joint or something."

Lurleen punched me in the face, hard, twice.

She shone her lavender eye-beams across the cave floor. "Hey Babs, has my hubby got anything left?"

Geezer had his mouth full. He was playing for time.

"Are you joking?" My wife pushed him away.

"In that case, are you thinking what I'm thinking?"

"Let's go."

"But girls," Geezer sounded meek. "Just a…"

Babette smacked him. His head spun. He fell down

and lay still.

"Get the keys to their bikes," Babette said.

"You can't handle that heavy old hog. Please…"

The world went black. Life was painful. The ladies riffled through our leathers, then a pair of motorcycles rode off into the night.

***

Geezer helped me up after what seemed like a long, long time. He was shaking, bad. "Can you believe it?"

"I was there, wasn't I?"

"Well, we got what we wanted, didn't we?"

"Right. Now how're we gonna get home?"

"Walk, I guess."

***

Two Death Jesters gave us a lift on the main road. Riding behind some greasy slob gave me a new perspective on Babette's existence. I resolved to be a better man, and buy her her own bike.

The guy shouted over the wind. "You guys headed to the gang bang?"

"What gang bang?"

"At Mother's. Couple chicks gone completely crazy."

"Oh. Far out."

There were many bikes parked out in front of Mother's, and more headed in from all directions. Whoops and hollers split the air. My '48 Knucklehead was crashed into a garbage dumpster. Geezer's

Indian was plowed into a car parked out front.

We pushed our way inside. Bikers swarmed like a cloud of leather flies around our wives, who were having the time of their lives. There was nothing to do but wait in line and watch.

"Uh, look man, that's my old lady there," I said to the dude ahead. "Mind if I cut in front of you?"

"No way, bro."

Geezer tapped my shoulder. "That stuff has to wear off sometime."

As soon as it was our turn, it did.

"Help! Rape! Somebody call the cops!"

The guy behind us said, "Oh yeah, I'm a cop."

The guy standing next to him said, "Me too."

Everyone else scattered. The cops clobbered us with their billy clubs, and snapped on the cuffs. A paddy wagon came. Tires squealed, sirens wailed.

Did our wives press charges? You bet your ass they did, bro.

Lube Job

The operator sounded much too cheerful. "P.J. Factory! How may I direct your call?"

Mick Stiff nearly hung up on her. He was looking for regular employment, willing to try a different line of work, but he wasn't ready to hit an assembly line, especially not in a sweatshop that produced pyjamas. Mick was more the sleep-in-your-undershirt type. But the guy who'd told him to call didn't sound like he was offering a clock-punch Joe Lunchpail type of job. The guy had stars in his eyes. Mick held the line.

"How soon can you get over here?"

Mick was used to being asked how many inches he had, or if he ever had problems getting wood. This was refreshing. He got the address and made it over to the P.J. Factory in under an hour.

"Thing is," the guy said, "most guys don't even wanna look at their old ladies after they've delivered. But that's where you come in, baby. I saw your loop–the fuck was it called–Milkin' Mamas. You were brilliant."

"Thanks," Mick Stiff said with shudder. He'd shot that lactation stroker under severe economic duress.

"You're a natural, kid. Most men never realize that milkers are the richest source of the most precious substance on Earth."

"Yeah? You can get crude oil from 'em?"

"No, you...well, actually, sorta...kid. Sorta. I'm talking about pussy juice."

"Huh?"

"That's our motto: We got a use for pussy juice."

"Uh, OK, but what's this job you were telling me about?"

"Well, that's our other motto: We milk it out of 'em!"

"Milk out of 'em...what?"

"Why, the pussy juice, you...Look, I'm gonna give you a shot. Ready to work hard?"

"Working hard's never been a problem, mister, but I still don't..."

"Maybe it's better if I show you, kid. Let's hit the production floor."

***

The P.J. plant didn't look like the usual factory. Mick Stiff's first glimpse of industry was what sent him screaming into the porn biz. But the porn biz had changed. There was too much competition. Stud fees had sunk to laughable levels, but there was no shortage of young guys who wanted a spot on the wet screen. The P.J. Factory looked soft. The light was low, the heat was on high, New Age muzak oozed from concealed speakers. There were nude women spread all over the place, leafing through magazines. They looked as though they'd been run through a stretching, softening machine. The P.J. Factory boss saw how Mick stared at them.

"Big tits, that's our motto!"

"You sure got a lot of mottoes here, Mr…"

"You wanna be a wise-ass, kid? Or do you wanna milk pussy juice?"

"Show me what I'm supposed to do."

"The job's a hands-on affair." The boss grabbed a soft blonde and gave her ass a swat. "Right, toots: assume the position. You'll be working with Nick, here."

"Mick. Mick Stiff."

She didn't bat an eyelash. She'd never heard of Mick Stiff before. She got on her hands and knees on a padded coffee-table, spread wide and looked back over her shoulder at Mick. Her nipples were leaking already.

"Ready when you are, gorgeous," she said, in a husky voice. "Shouldn't take me long."

The signs of recent motherhood were all there. Mick tried to put the traumatic images out of his head: the blood, the smell, the screams. The big blonde before him wiggled her hips. Mick dropped his pants, grabbed her ass and discreetly drooled down her crack. "Courtesy lube" is the professional term.

"Uh-unh, kid. You got the wrong idea. You're starting off at the wrong end. Remember our motto: We *milk* it out of 'em!"

Mick Stiff shuddered once again, but his coworker didn't seem to notice. He moved around to her front end and, before he could even lay hands on her, she immediately sucked his cock into her mouth.

Totally unfazed, he huffed into his palms, rubbing them both together. "Courtesy prep", he said to no one in particular

Then slowly, gently, he reached down and began to milk her.

Hot jets of cream soon began to spurt into a hole in the milking table. There was a distinct barnyard ambiance as the fluid hit the metal container.

"That's the way to work her, kid! What'd I say? You're a natural. Keep goin' while I get The Extractor. This one's a squirter from *both* ends!"

Mick kneaded her nipples, squeezed them down and wringed them off, just like his Uncle Olaf used to do on the farm back home in Wisconsin. She squirmed, bucked her hips as she began fingering herself from behind. Mick had been in the porn biz long enough to sense an impending gusher.

"Yah! Just in the nick of time!"

The blonde groaned against Mick's cock as she took deep down into her throat. Totally unfazed, he just kept right on milking those tits.

Soon enough, the juices were bursting from her back end as well. Mick couldn't believe she wasn't pissing. He looked at The Extractor – a black rubber accordion hose that ran into some kind of atomic vacuum cleaner contraption. The other end of the hose was attached to the blonde's gushing pussy. Lights blinked and needles jerked with sounds from a doomsday pinball machine.

"Whoa, stud. You got her going full throttle in no

time flat. But here's where we separate the men from the boys. Now, you do her tits."

Mick withdrew on command. No need for further courtesy lube. He mounted her cleavage and got to work.

"Wuh!" she said. "Wuh-uh-uh!"

"Easy, girl."

"Wuh! Wuh-huh-huh-uh! Nnnnngh—GOD!"

The Extractor blew like an air raid siren. Machine and lactating woman both went *WOOP WOOP WOOP* with alarm.

"Kid! You filled the tank! With *one* milker!"

The other nude women on the production floor drifted over to see what Mick Stiff was doing to their colleague.

"Don't crowd him," the boss said. "Everyone gets a turn. We're gonna run double shifts, if the new kid's up to it. How you doin' there, by the way, Rick?"

"That's Mick. And I'm doing fine. Ready for another, if you think this one's had enough. I can handle two, if it's not against company policy."

"Mick...Mick! Where you been all my life?"

After brief two-way preliminaries, Mick arranged the milkers belly-to-belly on the Extractor Table and worked them hard.

"You're a genius, kid! You're the fucking Mozart of milk! You are the Marcel Proust of pussy juice!"

"Boss, I'm gonna shoot. Can't hold off much longer."

"Go ahead, boy. Girls, get in there and help my new partner cum, for chrissakes!"

Instantly, Mick Stiff vanished into a pile of pink.

***

The P.J. Factory's executive lounge was a pair of stained recliners near a fridge that contained several six-packs of beer. A black-and-white TV showed an ice hockey game with the sound off. The silence bothered Mick.

"Uh, whuddaya *do* with all that pussy juice, boss?"

"What do I do with the pussy juice? What...why you... what the fuck do you care what I do with it?"

A Hard Case

My secretary fired me.

Detective stories usually begin: We'd been dry-humping on the couch in my office when my secretary said she wanted to go all the way. But here we go instead:

"You haven't paid me in weeks. You haven't had a new case in months. The cases you've got are stone cold dead. You're the worst detective in world. You couldn't detect stink in a garbage dump."

She slammed the door so hard it broke the etched glass panel the last sign painter in town had recently enlivened with my agency's logo.

The phone rang when I was about to call it a day. My secretary was gone. I answered.

"Sloane Investigations, Ned Sloane speaking."

"You the D-d-divorce D-d-detective?"

Wanda, my former secretary, had placed an ad in the local paper. She'd gone to art school for a bit, and claimed her linked-D logo illustrated the concept that we specialize in divorce cases. Other investigators won't touch them any more.

"Sir, you either have a stammer or you're a poor reader. I'm the Double-D Divorce Detective. I only handle cases where the unfaithful party is stacked.

You got a case for me?"

"Oh boy, do I ever. My Doris—that is, she used to be my Doris—has big'uns. That's how come we wound up together in the first place. Couldn't keep my mitts offa her."

Whoever was on the other end of the line was about to cry. A lost pair of big tits is tragic. I thought about my ex-secretary, Wanda. Private eyes are obliged to grope their girls Friday, but I'd never gotten grabby with her. Not much to grab. Just like my ex-wife. Meanwhile, the new client sobbed, sniffled and gasped for breath.

"Pull yourself together, sir. So, you think your wife's been unfaithful."

"She might've been, but the thing is, she's run away, with all our money. I mean, all *my* money!"

"Now that's serious, Mister..."

"Frawley. Odom Frawley. Any chance you'd work this job pro bono? That means for free, doesn't it?"

"Mr. Frawley, if you look at the ad's fine print, it states that I work pro boner. Show me a snapshot of your wife, preferably nude. If she's hot, I'll take the case. For a hundred bucks a day, plus expenses."

"That sounds awful cheap."

"Hey, whatever you say bud."

Frawley said he had several of pictures of his wife with no clothes on.

***

Doris Frawley was my kind of case. In one of my client's home photos, she was being measured for a new brassiere.

Frawley wrung his gnarled hands. She'd left him with barely a dime, he said. He still had to make payments on the car she'd driven off in, still had to pay the rent, and still had to take care of his elderly mother. I scribbled down where his wife went shopping, who her friends were, etc.

"Did she have a job?"

"Part-time stuff—waitressing, usually. She made good tips."

"How much did she take? Is it possible she has a bank account you don't know about?"

He shook his head. "She has no head for finance. And less than a thousand, I'd say. But it's all I had."

"When did she leave?"

"Two days ago. I kept thinking she'd be back."

His eyes welled up at the notion.

"This doesn't look good," I said, and spelled it out for him. His runaway wife had a car and plenty of gas money. Frawley had waited over 48 hours before he took action. She could be almost anywhere in the USA.

I told him to go home, and I'd do what I could.

"Leave the pictures of your wife."

From my second-floor office window, I watched him walk away, eyes on the pavement, shoulders hunched, hands in his empty pockets. I felt bad for the guy.

As soon as he was out of sight, I spread the pictures of Doris Frawley out across my desk and did what I could.

***

I hadn't been exactly straight with the client. I had a hunch where his wife was. There aren't too many places a busty woman with no head for figures and less than a thousand bucks in her purse can go.

So I drove over the hill for a slog through Topless Los Angeles.

Doris Frawley was the kind of woman who could get bar patrons to order cases of champagne with a whisper in the ear, given her natural assets. I showed her picture to managers, bouncers, and sweaty women on their breaks. "Hell, she'd put most of us out of a job," one of the topless ladies said.

Nobody on Western Avenue had seen Doris Frawley.

Sunset Strip looks like a glittering step up, but it's only further West, with parking lots for customers. And the dancers go all the way.

They serve ginger ale at places like the Tits Mahal. Nude women and alcohol don't mix, in that part of the world. Doris Frawley was another blank in Nude Los Angeles.

High-dollar soda-pops turned to gold when I headed back to the Valley. Some former Sheriffs Dept colleagues had set up a roadblock on Cahuenga Pass and were administering the breathalyzer to all passing motorists. Sheriff Johnson Brown leant his beer gut against my car door.

"Hot damn. Ned Sloane, the lawman who thought he could go it alone. Check the car. Check the clothes. You were doing better when you wore a badge. And now: have you been drinking, sir?"

"Not me. I'm working undercover. Wave me through."

"What kinda case you on? Lost pet?"

"A woman ran away from her husband."

"What's she look like?"

"Blonde, big in the chest."

"Like, how big?"

Brown whistled when he saw the picture. Sheriffs Dimshaw, Pettet and Cluskey shambled over.

"I'm gonna turn in my badge and gun tomorrow," Cluskey said.

"Take it easy," Brown said. "Sloane was spotted in several titty bars earlier this evening. He's unemployed, got nowhere else to go. Soon as this sobriety check bullshit's over, I'm gonna investigate whether he exposed himself to any strippers, or behaved otherwise indecently."

He waved me through with an obscene hand signal.

A gesture in a rearview mirror sparked intuition. Doris Frawley had hardcore appeal. That sort of talent leads to X-rated movies, which mean big bucks to those who produce them. Adult entertainment comes from North Hollywood, these days.

And I was headed in that direction anyway.

***

North Hollywood's a sleepy little town, especially at night.

All the gates were closed, the shutters down. No sign of life at any of the major adult studios, where on-camera love was usually more of a day job.

The head honchos at those porn factories were all interchangeable oily, overweight men. I'd rousted all of them on various occasions when I was still with the Sheriffs Dept. They ratted each other out like clockwork when pre-production dope deals went sour, or if a stacked or well-hung corpse turned up somewhere.

There was another adult film presence in North Hollywood, however, a phantom outfit known only as Project X. Their main client was rumored to be the United States' government.

The location of Project X's headquarters was a mystery in itself.

The car's hood ornament, a blindfolded woman in a windswept toga, guided me down the boulevards, avenues and alleys. North Hollywood memories flooded in through the speckled windshield. There was the high school, the public library, the swimming pool where girls once wore their first bikinis and boys first learned what a broken heart feels like. The drive-in hamburger restaurant where the waitresses hopped cars on roller skates. The drive-in movie theater where Senior Class President Jane Waddell said she was...

The green sign at the intersection of Xavier Ave and Exacerbation Blvd flashed in the headlights and rang a spooky bell. A red moon hung low in the sky and leered at the lifeless world below. A black X hand-painted on a busted plywood door through a low wall seemed to mark the spot.

Project X, if that's what the building was, didn't look like a movie lot. Anyone who drove by would've mistaken the place for a bush league chemical plant or a futuristic bakery. Everything was neat and white. On the outside, at least.

There was no barbed wire, no guard towers, no sentries posted. I parked and slithered back through the shadows to investigate.

There was a dumpster in the alley. Even if a garbage-dive in the dark didn't yield Doris Frawley's exsanguinated corpse, there might be factory reject DVDs or leftover raw footage. Jane Waddell might've turned into one of those North Hollywood housewives who earned extra housekeeping money with their clothes off, in conjunction with strange men, under hot lights.

A light burned on the second floor of the two-story building, invisible from the street. The lit window was closed, but a muffled scream came through, followed by moans. The voice, though deep, was unmistakably a woman's.

***

Someone scratched a match and lit a cigarette.

"May I help you, sir?"

The big man didn't really seem like the helpful type.

"My cat ran away," I said.

"That's too bad. But there aren't any cats around here."

Another gooey moan slid out from the window above.

"Funny," I said. "Sounds just like her."

"You said cat. *That's* pussy."

"Never heard of Women's Lib around here, huh."

"That's the professional term for female performers, in our business. Like they say 'talent' in the other, fabulous Hollywood. Now kindly get lost, before I call security."

"Just a moment. Is this Project X?"

"Ex-actly."

"You produce adult entertainment."

"We do."

"Is it true your main client is the United States' government?"

"That, I can neither confirm nor deny."

"Wait, did I say I was looking for a cat? I meant, I'm looking for a job."

He puffed deeply. "Let's see what you got."

He shook his head when I pulled my jacket aside to

show the butt of my .38. "We already have a night watchman, somewhere. But we're always interested in new, uh, talent."

"Oh," I said. "You mean, right out here in the alley?"

"You wanna turn pro? Then you'd better be ready to go at the drop of a hat."

He wasn't wearing a hat, even though the North Hollywood night was unseasonably cool.

"Tell me what honesty means, to you," he said.

"An honest person," I replied, "like a heartfelt statement, is open and unadorned."

"All right. Come on in for a screen test."

He ground out his cigarette in the beaten earth of the alley.

Stage jitters set in, then faded. The set-up at Project X was Spartan, but in an unexpected way. We went down a neon-lit hallway lined on one side with shelves of books and LP records. The walls on the other side were covered with black-and-white photographs of writers, painters, composers. Thomas Mann was prominent, in a gold frame.

The producer, if that's who the man was, opened a door and we entered a spacious, dimly lit room.

Doris Frawley was in there. She was nude, sprawled on a battered leather armchair under a brass lamp, immersed in reading *The Magic Mountain*.

"A far more violent novel than most people imagine," the producer said. "And more erotic than most readers care to remember."

***

The scene was macabre. A beautiful woman held prisoner by the book in her lap.

"This some new kind of torture?"

The guy who'd led me into Project X HQ hadn't taken my gun. No security goons had appeared. No cameras whirred, no hot lights shone, no microphones listened in, or at least it didn't feel that way.

"Are you kidding? She barged in here and offered us a cool grand if we'd take her on," he said. "We don't usually go for mercenaries, but we gave her a chance. We want performers with souls. The other outfits extrude more than enough feed for the masses. We go deeper."

Doris Frawley looked up, annoyed. "This was supposed to be a break. If you're going to talk, I'll go read in the commissary."

"Sorry, toots." The man herded me through a door off to the side, into a small soundproofed room. "Take a seat," he said. The director's chair in the corner had a stack of books beside it. "Get ready for your scene."

"What'm I supposed to do?"

"You're the detective. Take all the time you need." He closed the door, quietly as he left.

At the top of the book-pile was Daniel Fuchs' *The Golden West*, a love song to Los Angeles. Happiness radiated from solid blocks of print that looked like home.

A woman with bright red hair stuck her head in the

door, winked, and left me alone. That might've been some sort of movie-set signal. I ignored it, picked up F. Scott Fitzgerald's *The Pat Hobby Stories*. Time passed seamlessly.

The light in the room dimmed a shade or two. Fresh air came in from an invisible vent somewhere.

The crew had lost its patience. The producer, or director, whatever he was, came back in. He tossed Jim Thompson's *Savage Night* at me, somewhat painfully. "Here. Give this the once-over, and then let's go."

Not a long story, but a hard one to read.

The light went all the way out.

Music oozed from under the wooden door, heavy on the vibraphones and drums. Doris Frawley knocked, entered, shimmied over to where I was. She took my hand. We went out of the reading room into the light.

'This is a dream,' I thought, and then, 'this isn't a dream.'

Whatever we did on that blindingly lit set had purpose. It was up to us to find out what the action meant. We went deep, and then we went deeper. There was no bottom.

Someone yelled, "Cut!"

Doris didn't even open her eyes.

"We don't want to cut," she said. "We want to bring everything together..."

Whoever had the megaphone said, "Roll on!"

***

"Camera meltdown. Break!"

The words tunneled in through a thick fog. Where and why was life going on? Who revealed its secret? Whoever I was never wanted whatever had happened to end, but it ended anyway.

Life is like that.

Other times, you get stuck in the wrong life for too long.

Someone threw a blanket over my shoulders. That meant I had shoulders. Or maybe it was a towel. Whatever it was felt soft. Life didn't have to be hard. Not all the time.

The world was warm, and dark. The lights had burned so bright. Light needs a rest, too. The stars close their eyes when the day starts.

The light spoke itself alive. "Think you can give us another take in about half an hour?"

"How 'bout half a minute?"

"Stand by."

Life doesn't stand by. Life moves through space and time. Life finishes, especially when you don't want it to.

The bright lights blazed once again.

"There you are."

The soft voice cut through the glare. A touch that meant another life was there. Everything became clear again.

"Okay, now do the scene where you..." the big voice was unsure. "Just, do whatever you want."

Another facet of the mystery dazzled. The director knew what we were supposed to do together in the light. He just couldn't put it into words at the moment. But that didn't matter. All that mattered was out there in the light.

Light-years flew by in all directions and exploded in liquid heat.

"Got it. That's a wrap."

Whichever world this was grew darker and cooler. Time flowed. Breathe in, breathe out. Someone said, "Listen, you can't stay here. We need to clear the set for the maintenance crew."

You find a place where you want to be and then you have to leave. The clothes neatly folded on a folding chair seemed to fit. I still knew how to put them on. The gun was a leftover from the wrong job. "I don't want this anymore," I said, and handed it over to a young woman with a clipboard at her breast.

"I'll take care of it," she said.

Doris had a car outside. The motor started with no fuss. She let it warm up.

"Are you from Mexico?"

Usually I was the one who asked questions. The answers were for people who had problems in their lives that made them unhappy. My job was to change that. Or that's what I thought the job was. "I speak English," I said, eventually.

She put the car in gear and crawled out of Project X's lot. The words welded onto the gate sounded familiar.

"Work makes you free," Doris Frawley said. "At least here it does."

A green light came on and we drove off together into the North Hollywood night.

A blue light came on, and another one, too bright, both headed in the wrong direction. A siren yawped. We stopped.

"Get outta the car," a too-loud voice said. "With your hands up."

***

The voice was familiar, as was the tone Sheriffs Dept bulls use on people caught in the misery light. I got outta the car, hands up as instructed.

"Turn around." Sheriff Johnson Brown went heavy on the get-in-the-position judo and frisked hard.

"Where's your gun?" he said.

"Gone," I said. "Didn't need it anymore."

"Your former secretary called to report that your private investigator license expired."

Wanda always said I was a rotten detective, but dates and bureaucracy were an electron cloud spinning out of control in another, distant dimension.

"Things've changed," I said. "I work for the government now."

"Oh yeah? Then who's this ginch?" Sheriff Brown shone his heavy flashlight on Doris behind the wheel.

"She looks like the wrong side of a divorce case to me. Which means you're operating illegally.'"

"She's my new partner."

Doris flashed a Project X badge, which gleamed golden.

"She drives better than you, too," I said.

Sheriff Brown saw his party was pooped and threw in a surreptitious kidney punch. A call crackled in on the squad car's radio. There was a hostage situation at the Nursing Academy.

Sheriff Pettet said, "We'd better go, chief."

Their unmarked prowler crunched the gravel and broken glass and faded away.

Doris lit a cigarette, but then crushed it out in the ashtray.

We drove to a beach in Ventura County. The sun came up behind us. The Pacific waves lived up to their name and reputation. We went in, with our clothes off. The day finished with a green flash at a point where the world was a blue line and the sky was a pink infinity.

Time to go back to work at Project X.

The last detail of a misspent career in private investigation was a courtesy call to a former client.

"Mr Frawley, I found your wife."

"Oh? Hey, that's great. When..."

"But that's only because you lost her."

"Huh? Never had no complaints from any other..."

"She'll send you a check for what she borrowed to fund her escape from a nowhere life."

"But how…"

"When's the last time you did something for your country, Frawley? Think of it that way."

I hung up the phone.

www.ingramcontent.com/pod-product-compliance
Lightning Source LLC
Chambersburg PA
CBHW051224160726
47994CB00002B/743